GATE OF TORMENT

Hell Gates – Book One

V.C. Marello

Published by Relative Books

https://relativebooks.com

"There is no fear in love; but perfect love casteth out fear: because fear hath torment..."

—1 JOHN 4:18 (KJV)

To my father who allowed me, at the age of seven, to watch old campy British horror movies all day long on Saturdays. To this day, I continue to sleep with the covers over my head.

admin@relativebooks.com

Published by Relative Books
1050 Glenbrook Way, Ste. 480-219, Hendersonville, TN 37075
https://www.relativebooks.com

This book is a work of fiction. Names, characters, places, and incidents either are products of the author's imagination or are used fictitiously. Any resemblance to actual persons, living or dead, events, or locales is entirely coincidental.

Editor: J.K. Gray

Book Cover designed by Relative Books
Cover Images:
ID 4361298 © Hangyanyee | Dreamstime.com (Dragon Doorknob)
ID 100524110 © Andrei Shupilo | Dreamstime.com (Green Flames)

Published in the United States of America
ISBN: 978-1-7346379-1-5 (Print)

CONTENTS

CHAPTER 1

Night Crew

The gigantic neon sign, *Tony's Food Mart*, blazed like a beacon in the night above the deserted parking lot. Behind the sign, perched high on a cliff, stood the United States Mint building silhouetted by a full moon. The night was cool, crisp, and unusually clear for San Francisco. No trace of fog anywhere. A rusty cargo van bounced into the empty parking lot, avoiding several stray grocery carts scattered about while continuing towards the rear of the store.

Several grungy, oily rats scurried into the grimy loading dock, fleeing for their lives as the van zoomed by. Rounding the corner, the van passed several overstuffed garbage bins, then skidded to a stop next to the store's back door. The eerie stillness of the night returned quickly, disrupted only by the steam from the engine's cracked head.

The back door swung open, and Mike Hanson darted out, pulling an empty grocery dolly with him. His olive-colored grocery apron secured tightly around him, which accentuated his brawny chest and broad shoulders. Mike's closely cropped chestnut hair was the same hairstyle he continued to wear even after leaving the army two years ago. He did not like the style himself, but his fiancée did and that is all that mattered to him. He approached the back of the van and stopped to scan the area. After confirming that no one else was around, he opened the back doors.

Luis and Jerry sprinted out from the rear entrance. Jerry attempted to light Luis' cigarette, but stumbled, dropping his lighter into the back of the van. Jerry's short stubby legs never fit him properly, so regular length pants often caused him to trip over himself. While in the Army, he was constantly criticized for looking sloppy and unkempt. His oily black curls and five o'clock shadow, which seemed to appear again shortly after he finished shaving, did nothing to improve his image.

"Jesus Christ!" yelled Mike, as he quickly picked up the lighter from the top of a box of bananas. "Jerry, you're so fucking stupid."

"All the time if you asked me," snickered Luis, as the unlit cigarette barely clung to his lips as he talked. Luis' demeanor was stereotypical to the background story he had told everyone. He painted himself as a hard-core gang banger from the slums of Oakland who had killed his best friend just to join them. He had a collection of tattoos on both of his arms and legs, along with an outlandish story associated with each one. Luis wanted to be feared, but deep down it was the respect from others that he truly sought. In most cases, no one took him seriously and thought he was a loudmouth fool.

Mike knew better. He knew Luis' game as he himself was currently playing one as well; creating a role that truly was not him. He hid the truth to protect himself and the ones he loved by refraining from forming any emotional bonds with those around him.

Luis was really the polar opposite of the image he sought to project. He was highly intelligent and from an affluent family in the Oakland community. He had grown up in the Oakland hills, looking down upon the gangbangers, and sought to emulate. He had never been the bone-headed badass he was now attempting to portray, especially while serving in the U.S. Army.

Mike stared momentarily at the two pathetic guys that stood before him. Buddies. He thought about that for a second. Maybe at one time they were buddies, but no longer and definitely not after they complete their work at this grocery store. At first, he had reservations about asking these two to join him on this job, but all guilt had evaporated as his nightmares intensified since returning to civilian life.

Just over two years ago, these two "buddies" had left Mike and three other soldiers for dead alongside a road in Afghanistan. They were hit by an IED during their patrol. The sun, high overhead, scorched everything. They were the only living creatures for miles. While deployed, their friendship had been tight. They had to be close and function as a team just to survive. It was their last week in this hellhole and they had promised to watch each other's backs until their last day. No one wanted to get killed a week before their tour ended and returned to civilian life.

The vivid memories were a constant part of Mike's consciousness, fueling his anger. Fucking cowards! You two chickened out, abandoned us without even checking to see if we were still alive. Normally, he could keep the intensity at bay. Occasionally, it would escape. At that moment, a look of pure rage flickered across his face.

"You okay, Mikey?" asked Luis. He had seen that sinister look before on Mike's face. The first time was when Mike limped into camp shortly after Luis and Jerry had returned from their patrol. They had left them all there, blown apart by a land mine. They thought their buddy was dead, along with the grunts who had just arrived a few weeks earlier.

Luis had noticed the same expression on Mike's face several times since they returned home. It was an icy, callous look that tugged at Luis' soul and it frightened him. Luis thought about why he allowed Mike to talk him into this ridiculous job. Greed, of course. That's all Luis thought about since his parents cut him off from any financial support. He had to live with Jerry since returning to the States because his family refused to accept him back.

"Come on, ladies!" Mike snapped. "Grab those boxes and bags. We probably won't need it all, but better to have more than not enough. Just like old times."

"There's enough C4 here to blow the Mint building into the bay," remarked Luis as he lifted the top off one of the two banana boxes revealing the sticks of dynamite packed inside. "Dynamite? Who uses dynamite nowadays? Maybe we'll get it to roll off the cliff if we're lucky."

"Who cares how much we use, just as long as we get this over with. I'd like to ditch this grocery clerk gig. It's been three months and working night-crew is feeling like an actual job," whined Jerry.

"Stop bitching and get this stuff down into the basement. It's the best I could do on short notice." Mike struggled to keep his temper under control with these saps.

For the last two years, the nightmares had mercilessly tormented him. Images of babies and small children blown to pieces, their lifeless faces staring directly into his eyes as he walked through the massacre. Those eyes looked deep into his soul and saw the veritable monster he had become. He enjoyed killing people. It became a game to him, watching his victims run away or be unaware he was about to pull the trigger and end their lives. Would he do it swift and clean or down and dirty, starting at an extremity to slow them down first, then shoot them again and again, moving closer to their head or heart? These images haunted him more and more every day until he put into action the agreement he had made. They subsided once he began working at this store.

Though the haunting dreams seemed to diminish a bit, he would never be completely free of them until he finished the job. The images of himself dying in a hole in the desert were intermixed among those of his victims. He even felt the warm sensation of his own blood running down from his head, along his neck, and dripping out into the sand. Flashes of the other soldiers' body parts appeared and then morphed into a small child's mangled body. These flashes confused Mike and clouded his judgement. He vowed he would get out of that hole and back to his fiancée—no matter what he had to sacrifice.

His stomach twisted and ached when he arrived at work each night and looked at these two cowards. They had betrayed his friendship, turned their backs on him, but now he worked right next to them. The memories of that day flared up every time he heard one of them laugh or slap him on the shoulder. The agony of dragging his bloody, shattered body along the road back to base was etched deeply into his mind. His worst nightmare-dying alone in the desert-was now almost a reality. He yearned for it all to stop. Stop now. It was a miracle, everyone said, as they rushed him to the medical tent. Right, a miracle indeed. If they only knew the price he paid to continue living beyond that fateful day. Mike grinned. Soon his two ex-buddies would learn just what kind of sacrifice was made.

His two so-called comrades pushed the overloaded cart into the store. The boxes appeared to be filled with produce while the two bags were burlap potato sacks. Mike looked back into the van at the driver.

The driver, dressed all in black with a hood pulled up over his head, kept his gloved hands on the steering wheel the entire time. The driver never turned around.

"Take off, Harry. We've got it from here. I'll call you tomorrow if I have any good news to report.

Now get out of here." The driver raised his hand in acknowledgement as Mike shut the rear doors. The van immediately pulled away and faded into the night.

As Mike secured the store's back door, he opened it once again and gazed up at the U.S. Mint building. "Tonight, my friend, I hope we finally get to see what you've been hiding deep in those bowels of this hill. I will fulfill my promise to you. You better fulfill yours." He paused a moment longer as if waiting for a response or a signal from the building. Nothing. Only silence greeted him, so he closed the door.

Luis and Jerry had pushed the dolly onto the freight elevator and impatiently stared back at Mike. Luis sat on top of the supplies while Jerry leaned against the side wall of the elevator, pantomiming pushing the down button.

Mike sprinted over while flipping them off. As long as Mike had known them, they had always been impatient. They had met the first day of boot camp and bonded immediately. Bonded not because they had common interests, mind you, but what united them was that each of them was scared shitless. They stayed together to overcome the fear of being alone in the strange oppressive environment that was basic training.

His phone chirped as soon as he stepped into the elevator. He looked at the caller ID as he dug the phone out of his shirt pocket.

"Crap! It's the boss. I'd better answer, or he'll come down here in person tonight and just slow us down." He stepped off the elevator and slowly started pacing in a circle next to some grocery pallets. "Hey Mr. Helovich, what's up?" The screaming, guttural voice of the store manager came through the phone. Mike moved it away from his face as if he expected some spittle to fly out of the phone. "Yes, we will get everything done tonight. The store will look great for you in the morning. Yes, for the customers too."

Mike noticed that Luis and Jerry continued to just stare at him as he remained walking in a circle. He pointed to the ground several times before the two idiots understood his gestures. Jerry pushed the button, and the door closed. The hydraulic humming of the elevator kicked in, and they descended into the basement.

"Yes, I know, sir," responded Mike. "You are taking a chance on us Vets to do a superb job and you're expecting us to be just as dedicated to our jobs as we were to our country." Although Mike's voice remained calm, what Mr. Helovich could not see was Mike's eyes rolling up into his head. He released a quick round-kick several times into a pallet of dog food. One bag ripped open, spilling some nuggets out onto the floor. He just shook his head and resumed pacing. "My team and I have been here for over three months now. Have we let you down yet?" Mike waited a couple of seconds and hearing only silence decided to continue. "Trust me, my guys don't do drugs and are hard workers, unlike your previous night crew."

That response seemed to satisfy Mr. Helovich as the next thing Mike heard from the cell phone was "Carry on", and then it went dead.

The store had a full-size basement, but the ceiling was low because of the water pipes and electrical wiring which ran haphazardly along most of it. This created a tiny space between the full pallets and the ceiling. It felt like a labyrinth in which one would have to carefully plan their path through the maze to find the desired grocery items. A couple of hand pallet jacks, several motorized pallet jacks, and some grocery dollies were scattered around the area.

The freight elevator descended slowly. When the hydraulic humming stopped, the doors sluggishly opened. Luis and Jerry had to manually lift the safety gate, then staggered off as they struggled to push the overloaded dolly out of the elevator.

They zigzagged through rows of grocery pallets, past a smaller freight elevator next to the Produce Department area. They then passed a large cardboard baler that looked like a rusty metal-munching mouth, which was currently wide open and waiting for its next feeding. They approached the back of the basement where a chain-link fence and gate blocked them from going any further.

The fenced-off area was for securing the most expensive inventory, such as cigarettes, alcohol, batteries, and film. Luis pulled out a key from under his apron and unlocked the padlock attached to the gate. He then held the gate open for Jerry, who fought to push the dolly into the secured area. Luis grabbed a motorized pallet jack and inserted it into the furthest pallet of the area's back corner.

He attempted to lift the pallet and pull it out as the stack of cigarettes on the pallet swayed. Luis slowed down the speed a bit to keep the boxes from falling off. He parked the pallet in the aisle just on the other side of the security fence.

Jerry, finally having some momentum with the dolly, maneuvered it into the space that Luis had just created. He removed a large canvas drape that hung on the brick wall, revealing a large hole.

A sudden loud ringing bell echoed throughout the basement. Both guys instinctively froze, looked up at the ceiling, then at each other.

"Load's here. Should we go up and help?" asked Jerry.

"Let Mikey handle it," responded Luis. "He never needs our help, and yet, he asked us to come along and help him with this job. And that job is to find the vault not to unload groceries."

Luis' fear of Mike only allowed him to talk crap about Mike to Jerry when Mike was not around. He would never do it if he thought Mike was nearby—too risky. The day Mike stumbled into camp, covered in blood and yet seemingly with no serious injuries from the blast, was the day Luis saw a darkness in Mike's eyes he had never seen before. After the explosion, Luis immediately turned the truck around and headed back to base.

Jerry tried to stop him. He wanted to get out and inspect the scene since sitting in the passenger seat had not allowed him to see any details. Luis yelled at him to shut up and just be happy they were still alive.

Luis often questioned himself: *what if he hadn't panicked? Hadn't ran away after witnessing body parts flying in all directions from the explosion?* Looking back on that day, he wished he had let Jerry get out and check it out for himself. Jerry would have seen that it was impossible that Mike had survived. Seeing the pools of blood and body parts littering the ground would surely have caused Jerry to fear Mike just as much as Luis did. It was an image that remained indelibly etched in his mind.

When Luis saw Mike enter the camp, he noticed Mike's uniform was shredded to pieces and barely covered his body—perhaps the dried blood from the other soldiers enabled what uniform remained to adhere to Mike's body.

Mike claimed the soldiers' bodies had shielded him from the blast and that he had been knocked out when he hit the ground. Luis could not remember the names of the other soldiers or even their faces. Worse yet, he didn't care. He was soon going to rotate back home, and they were just the FNG's–Fuckin' New Guys.

Somehow all three had survived and made it home, each pretending it was because they had each other's back. Luis and Mike returned home to the San Francisco Bay Area. Jerry followed Luis since his own hometown, Hanford, California, had nothing to offer him. No family or friends cared to see him. No girlfriends. No one. So, he shadowed Luis, since he knew Luis didn't mind having him around.

Luis and Jerry shared an apartment in the East Bay, while Mike was only a few miles away in San Francisco. Even though they lived in proximity to each other, Mike carefully avoided them. Mike always gave Jerry an excuse to why he couldn't meet up.

Luis never attempted to reach out to Mike and never encouraged Jerry to do so either. Being the friend in the middle all the time, Jerry hoped to restore their trust and friendship with Mike once again.

It was six months ago that Mike unexpectedly called Jerry. He let them know he had a job for both of them in San Francisco, if they were interested. Luis would never have considered getting involved with Mike again, but he couldn't hold down a steady job since he returned, only odd jobs here and there. Jerry worked as a Barista at a café on the corner by their apartment. It was simple work, but the pay low and tips rare. They both were looking for a quick way to earn a lot of money and that's when Mike showed up with his offer. They would be set for life if they just helped him out on this job. The offer seemed easy enough—no one to kill, nothing illegal since technically the vault was lost years ago. It was more like a treasure hunt.

The one thing Luis hated was that they had to pretend to be grocery clerks for the last three months. They needed to get into the basement of this store and start digging. Luis wanted to get his share and disappear from the Bay Area, his family, and especially from Mike.

"Let's go," commanded Luis. "We have real work to do. Leave the All-American Asshole to take care of the dairy delivery by himself."

Jerry grabbed two tactical headlamps from behind a box of cigarettes on a shelf next to the hole in the wall. He tossed one to Luis. They slipped them onto their heads, then lit the lights. Both started picking up supplies from the grocery dolly and headed into the pitch-black hole. Luis' slim build allowed him to pass easily through the tunnel, but Jerry was stocky. He struggled as the thickness around his stomach would bump against the uneven tunnel walls, and at times, he'd have to suck it in, to pass through.

They shuffled through the hand-carved tunnel, balancing the supplies in their arms, as dust rose from the uneven dirt floor. Eventually, Luis stepped out of the carved pathway, and moments later, the same tunnel spit Jerry out as he struggled to hold on to both boxes of dynamite. He dropped to one knee to keep himself from falling flat on the ground.

The tunnel opened into a vast void of darkness. Their headlamps revealed a wall of tile and brick in the distance. They stood in an abandoned train tunnel with the tracks running from the right to the left from where they entered. Their lights did not penetrate to the end of the tunnel in either direction. Cave-ins blocked both ends, though they could not see that yet. In the middle of the cavern, a couple of camping tables were setup and a variety of digging tools were scattered around them. Most appeared to be bent or broken.

Luis placed the bags filled with new digging tools on one of the two tables, then switched on a battery lantern hanging on a stand between the tables. It emitted enough light to illuminate most of the abandoned tunnel now, with only its farthest reaches still in darkness.

A large canary-colored smiley face, with coal-black eyes and rosy puckered lips, was painted on the wall opposite the smaller passage they had entered from the store basement. Between its lips, a hole had been chipped out. Jerry placed the two boxes of dynamite on the empty table.

"Bring that shit over here," demanded Luis.

"Why'd I have to carry this stuff? You're the expert."

"You're asking now? Isn't that a bit late? You already carried it this far."

Jerry reluctantly picked up the boxes again and placed them carefully on the ground in front of Luis and next to the smiley face.

"Pucker up, Baby. I've got a big surprise for you." Luis popped off the lid of one of the banana boxes full of dynamite. He picked up several sticks and slid them one by one into the small hole.

"How many do you think we'll need?" Jerry had always blindly followed Luis around without question, but he realized Luis did not always have the best judgement.

Luis had told Jerry that no one survived the blast, so he hadn't questioned him. But now, Jerry's guilt was eating away at him internally every time he looked at Mike. He hadn't been able to look Mike directly in the eye since, so when they talked, he focused on Mike's chin or perfect pearly teeth. Better yet, he would let Luis do the talking to Mike whenever possible. Jerry noticed Luis had pulled away from Mike. He figured Luis was dealing with his own guilt about the whole situation.

But all that changed when Mike reached out and asked them to join him on this job. It was an opportunity that would set them all up financially, and it wasn't per se illegal. He figured Mike must have forgiven them, though the incident had never been talked about among the three of them. Jerry felt working with Mike would help regain Mike's friendship and trust. At least, that's what he prayed would happen. Jerry repeated his question to Luis. "How many do you think we'll need?"

"As many sticks of dynamite as it takes to blast a hold large enough so we can stand up straight and proudly walk in and grab what's ours. This wall is thicker than usual. Also, I'm fed up with small spaces. Being bent over digging out that tunnel killed my back." Luis began grabbing sticks from the second banana box and continued feeding them into the smiley face's mouth. "Besides, the bigger the hole, the easier and quicker we can load it up and get it out of here."

Jerry thought about the response for a moment. Something didn't sound right. "Wait! Burn it up?"

"It's fucking gold, stupid! Not cash. It might melt a little, but it won't burn."

Jerry nodded in agreement and handed over the remaining two sticks of dynamite.

♦ ♦ ♦

The delivery door on the loading dock was rolled open. Three dairy pallets were lined up against the wall next to the freight elevator. Mike backed out of the truck and slowly maneuvered the last pallet of milk off as he attempted to keep the plastic milk crates from swaying. He turned the motorized jack towards the rest of the dairy pallets.

A crusty, geriatric, pot-belly truck driver sat at the delivery desk by the back door, smoking an almost non-existent stogie. He stood up and inspected the back of his trailer. "Looks like ya got 'em all, son," he said, around the stump of a cigar stuck in the corner of his mouth.

"Where's the paperwork? I'll sign it so you can be on your way. No need to go over the invoice. I'm sure it's all here." Mike positioned the pallet next to the rest of the dairy delivery and was about to lower it into position when a loud rumbling noise echoed through the building. The floor and walls quivered.

Both Mike and the old truck driver, surprised by the sudden shaking, stared at the last pallet of milk and watched as the crates swayed back and forth.

"Quick, get on the other side to steady it!" shouted Mike as he rushed to the opposite side of the pallet. Both men tried to keep the crates from falling over. The old trucker moved fast for his age. They stabilized the swaying crates, spilling no milk.

"Shit, that was close. Would have been a lot of milk to clean up. Ever see a guy crushed by falling milk crates? I have. Horrible sight. Not one I'd want to see ever again." The remnants of the cigar bounced on his lower lip.

"I've seen worse, I'm sure."

"What was that explosion?" asked the truck driver.

"Explosion? What explosion?" questioned Mike, even though he knew exactly what had occurred. He also knew the two idiots had used most, if not all, of the dynamite. He had to think of something quick and reasonable. "Oh, you mean the earthquake. They always sound like explosions around here. Old buildings like these. It's San Francisco. What do you expect? That was mild. A bigger one usually follows shortly afterwards." Mike threw that last bit in to cover the off chance there might be any dynamite left.

The truck driver's face paled. "Bigger, huh? Well, I'll see ya later." He walked over to the back of the truck and pulled up the metal bridge that was connecting the truck to the loading dock. He pulled down the truck's back door and walked hurriedly to the dock's side door.

"What about signing the paperwork?" asked Mike.

"I'll forge your name. That's fine." He spit out the cigar stub into the dock pit and slipped out the door before Mike could respond.

Mike sprinted over to the store's rolling door and pulled it down. He heard the truck engine start up and rev loudly as the truck pulled away, gears grinding.

He jogged towards the stairs that would bring him down to the store level but paused for a moment to look at the dairy pallets he had just unloaded. He checked his watch. There wasn't enough time. They would have to put the milk in the refrigerator later. He needed to get down into the basement and see what, if anything, remained of the two dimwits. He hopped down a couple of steps, reached the main store level, passed the freight elevator, and took the stairs down to the basement.

Mike rushed through the basement maze, then slowed down as he approached the hole in the far back wall and watched as smoke and dust drifted out.

If those two have collapsed the tunnel, I'll break their necks. His anger rose instantly with that thought. He passed the chain-linked gate as dust continued to flow out of the passage. Two dark masses stumbled out while coughing severely.

"I told you that was too much!" Jerry spewed dust from his lungs.

Mike grabbed Luis' headlamp and pulled it away from his head for a moment and then let it snap back. Luis was dazed. "Stupid Ass! You could have brought down the entire store and then we'd never get in there again."

Luis didn't react to Mike's physical or verbal attack.

Mike approached the hole in the wall, pausing for a second to grab a headlamp from the shelf. He turned on its light, then covered his mouth with his sleeve and disappeared into the dust-belching mouth of the hole.

In the abandoned train tunnel, Mike searched through the debris and eventually uncovered the lantern. He tapped it twice and after a couple of flashes, it finally stayed on. As he looked around, the thick cloud of dust hung suspended in the air. They would have to wait awhile for the particles to settle before visibility would improve.

Luis and Jerry followed Mike into the tunnel, covering their mouths to keep from breathing in any more of the floating grits.

"All the equipment is buried. This will set us back several days now! Why couldn't you just have waited for me?"

Jerry looked down at the ground, not daring to look Mike in the eye as he knew they had failed him again. "Sorry, really we are. But we just wanted to..."

"Mike? Mike!" whispered Luis at first, then was more commanding as his senses came back to him. "Mike! Turn off the damn lantern. Please?"

Mike stared at him for a moment. "What the hell?"

"Come on man, just turn it off for a second. Trust me, please."

Mike would never trust either of them, but it was the 'please' that caught him off guard. Luis had never used that word towards him or anyone else. So, Mike turned off the lantern but kept his other hand near the knife he always carried, in case either of them betrayed him.

Their eyes took a moment to adjust to the darkness. Through the dense air, an eerie, emerald luminescence appeared beyond the far wall where the smiley face had once been. Since the tile and cement wall no longer stood before them, carved stone steps which led upward could be seen just past the rubble. Along the path, small patches of glowing moss dotted the walls.

CHAPTER 2

The Emerald Path

The three men stood stock-still and stared at the passageway, their minds racing a mile a minute. What they saw erased all doubt; there truly was something hidden down here. They turned to each other and started laughing and slapping each other on the back as they expressed their excitement. They had finally reached what they were searching for. Mike bent down and unearthed a long-handled grub axe. He grabbed it, then headed along the path, at a slight incline.

Luis and Jerry frantically looked around for some type of digging tool. Luis found a flat-nosed shovel while Jerry reached into the debris and pulled out a small pickax. Luis grinned as he showed Jerry the shovel and chuckled, "Mine's bigger," he teased, then he chased after Mike who had already disappeared down the passageway.

Jerry looked at his puny pickax while he continued searching for a different tool, but to no avail. Not wanting to get left behind, he quickly jogged up the path in search of his buddies.

The three walked down the corridor, stepping over or around pieces of cement and brick which the blast had thrown along the path. The further they proceeded the less dust lingered in the air; even the debris from the blast had become sparse. The entire passage had a natural jagged stone formation except for the ground which had been smoothed out with steps carved right into the stone. There was no question. This was definitely a man-made path that led under the U.S. Mint. The air was stale. There was a heaviness as well, and the average person would easily mistake that feeling for the coolness in the tunnel, rather than the sinister presence that was gnawing at their souls.

As they continued, the iridescent green light intensified as more of the strange moss clung to the stone walls. It was bright enough now that they turned off their headlamps. The passage then leveled out, revealing an enormous, natural underground chamber. The same glowing moss now covered almost the entire walls and ceiling, yet the floor was remarkably clear.

Up to this point, they had remained silent, lost in their own thoughts about what they were going to find as they were drawn farther and farther into the chamber. The mysterious light seemed to block any worries or concerns about what might be ahead of them.

As they approached the far side, thirteen perfectly carved granite steps appeared. Each one was thirteen feet wide and thirteen inches high. At the top of the steps were three thirteen-foot-tall carved stone pillars. The outer two columns bore carvings of archangels staring at the middle column, which was that of a coiled dragon. Its head tilted downwards, glaring directly at anyone who dared to ascend those steps.

♦ ♦ ♦

An exquisite young Asian woman stood by the door of the subway car. She stared at the window's reflection watching, not herself, but the other passengers surrounding her as the train raced through the inky blackness of a tunnel. She wore a large brim hat with feathers and a soft, pink traveling dress.

It was a dress style from the early nineteen hundreds, or at least that is what Alan thought as he gazed at her from the other end of the railcar. He had seen a similar dress in a historical period movie a few weekends ago, which he ended up watching alone at an artsy movie theater off Market Street. His blind date hadn't returned from the restroom as the movie started, so he ended up watching the entire movie by himself. Then he walked home alone in the rain. So cliché, he thought. But typical of how all his dates usually ended.

He stood up, trying to make his way towards the Asian woman. There were so many other people on the train. He could not make out their faces, but he knew they were men and women. No matter how hard he focused on trying to see their faces, he never could. They remained blurry, except for the young Asian lady whose face he could see clearly. As she stared out the window, he saw her reflection and the despair in her eyes.

The lights in the railcar flickered, paused, then flickered again as they continued traveling through the tunnel. With each flash, Alan thought he was getting closer, but at the same time was always too far away to reach her, to touch her. He did not know why he needed to, but he had to save her. But from what? He studied her face carefully. His gut told him that her life was going to end at any moment. She knew it as well. But what was the danger? Who was she?

Alan did not know any of those answers, yet in his heart, he felt the urgency to protect her. He pushed the people aside, fighting to get closer. He looked over at her each time he pushed through a group, only to see that she was still beyond his reach. It was not making sense to him as he knew he should be next to her by now, and yet, each time he pushed through a group of passengers she was always the same distance from him.

The exit doors flew open, and huge fiery eyes flashed at the young lady. She screamed and turned towards Alan. "Save me! Save me, Alan!"

She knew his name, but how?

From the far end of the train where he had originally been sitting, an emerald dragon materialized and slithered past him. Like a monstrous snake, it wrapped itself around her.

Lavender lingered in the air shortly after the creature passed him. Lavender? Why am I smelling lavender? He thought.

Her eyes pleaded with him to do something, to help her somehow.

Alan leaped forward to grab her. As he flew through the air, a clawed hand reached in and snatched her. The dragon remained wrapped around her as the claw pulled her out of the train and into the darkness. Alan landed hard on the floor next to the open door. The wind whipped past him and a warm, pungent aroma stung his nostrils, causing him to jump to his feet just as the claw returned, grabbing him and pulling him into the void.

Alan jolted awake on the floor of his bedroom. Sweat dripped from his body and saturated his underwear. His breathing was heavy and labored. His heart was pumped up on adrenaline so much that he felt it would burst. He picked himself up off the floor and dragged his semi-naked body into the bathroom. The cold water felt incredible as he splashed it over his face. He looked in the mirror and noticed how flushed his face was, as if he had been out for a long day in the sun. He stuck his head out the open window to get some fresh air. He took several deep breaths to calm down. Still half-asleep, Alan did not notice the absence of the fog which usually smothered San Francisco, nor did he notice the full moon.

He fell back into bed and pulled the blankets all the way over his head, leaving only a small opening around his face so he could still breathe. When he was a child, he always slept that way when he was scared. His reasoning was that the monsters in the room couldn't find him or bite his head off if they could not see him. A childish solution. It was false security. He knew it, but it helped him fall back to sleep promptly.

◆ ◆ ◆

Across town from Alan's apartment, Grace, a delicate elderly Asian woman, bolted upright in her bed screaming. She held herself tight as she shivered; her body covered in sweat. The dark room illuminated faintly as a shaft of light entered the room from between the curtains and reflected on the wall next to her nightstand.

She crawled out of bed. Her form silhouetted as she approached the curtains. Peering out the window of her third-floor apartment, she looked across the street to where she had worked for so many years—Tony's Food Mart. The store's outrageously tall, aging neon sign was the primary source of the light invading her room. When she noticed the full moon, she checked the calendar hanging on the wall next to the window. April Eighteenth was circled. Her index finger touched that date and she whispered, "No." Then she tapped it again and again even harder and said loudly, "No!" Finally, she screamed, "No!" while slamming her fist on the entire calendar. Her hand trembled. "You will never escape on my watch as I promised my father!" Her left hand instinctively reached up and clutched a small emerald dragon pendant attached to a silver chain around her neck. She shuffled back to bed. She laid back down and was asleep before hitting the pillow. The dragon remained grasped firmly in her hand. A faint jade aura engulfed her body.

◆ ◆ ◆

"What the hell is this?" asked Luis as he inspected the steps, noticing that the glowing moss stayed clear of both the steps and the columns. Beyond the columns themselves, the emerald light continued to shimmer, but they could not see its source from where they stood.

"It's the entrance. We've reached our destination, boys," responded Mike confidently as he hopped up the steps.

Jerry stood back from the two of them as he inspected the line which separated the natural cavern from the carved marble entrance. "You said this was a secret entrance to the vault. This is a pretty big entrance to be a secret."

"It was 1906. The Great San Francisco Earthquake. Come on guys, I told you this before. The entrance is a secret because the hill collapsed and sealed it closed during the quake. It's been forgotten all these years. Look, this is where the guards were posted. The hill collapsed on top of it and created this cavern." Mike paced back and forth along the top of the steps while gesturing for them to come up. "Would you be happier if I called it the forgotten entrance? That's it! I present to you, my partners in crime, the forgotten entrance to the U.S. Mint's vault from 1906. Lost to all until tonight." Mike gestured again for them to come on up. Since they hesitated, he didn't wait. He just turned around and left.

Luis and Jerry scurried up the steps, racing each other to the top. They even shouldered each other a bit, but both gripped their ground and arrived at the top together. They laughed out loud while stopping to catch their breath, coughing out more of the lingering dust in their lungs.

CHAPTER 3

Surprise Guest

The glistening light source was not from the moss they had seen earlier, but emanated from a monolithic, weathered wooden Gate reinforced with iron bands. The Gate was seventy-seven feet back from the three columns. The walls and ceiling were smooth, covered with shiny white marble, which reflected the eerie green glow coming from the gate. Much of the floor was hidden with a dense layer of crunchy, dusty debris. Mike was more than halfway to the Gate but stopped to look back at his buddies and waited for them to catch up.

The imposing Gate was almost as high as the ceiling, and its two doors were each thirteen feet wide. An epic battle of angels and demons, humans and dragons, was carved into the doors. Good and

Evil intertwined in a never-ending battle. A large iron ring protruded from the head of a dragon about halfway up from the ground on both doors. In the center, where the two doors met, one side of the dragon's face depicted an angelic expression, while its opposite side depicted a demonic stare and devilish grin. The faces gaze, locked together by the closed doors, fell on the newcomers.

The rest of the wall surrounding the gate was marble, with illustrated symbols outlining the doors. These symbols emitted the identical emerald light that the moss radiated. Neither of the three men knew what the symbols meant.

"Boys, this is it!" proclaimed Mike as he wormed around various piles of rubble scattered about the perimeter of a small dried up marble pond. The pond had a smaller dead tree in its center. The debris he couldn't avoid crackled and crunched as he walked. "Our reward is just on the other side of these doors." Dust whirled up with each step he took and clung like little clouds lingering in the air.

Jerry walked cautiously as he approached, since the heavier debris now moaned and groaned with each step he took. "Thank god Luis didn't collapse this area, we'd never have found it."

Luis followed close behind Jerry as both hastened towards Mike and the shimmering gate.

"Mike, why's it glowing? Security sensors?" questioned Jerry.

Luis laughed. "Sure, Jerry. They had laser beams in 1906. You sure are stupid!"

"Exactly my point," replied Jerry. "There's something wrong here." Luis and Jerry both paused next to the empty pond, which was exactly in the center of the room.

Mike examined the source of the radiating light that cascaded over the gate and the symbols. "I think it's just the residue of the glowing moss."

"So, Mikey, what are you waiting for? Not scared, are you? Open it. Let's get the gold and get the hell out of here," challenged Luis, refusing to move any closer. Why was Mike hesitating? he thought. Something had changed. Mike's expression now was one of concern which he used to get when they first went out on patrol. Mike was physically showing that he was uneasy in this place though he tried to sound confident. Was Mike going to double cross them? No, he would never do that. Luis knew Mike always had a guilty mind whenever he had to shoot someone when it wasn't out of self-defense. Mike always struggled with hurting the innocent and often would shoot to miss on purpose, especially if there were children.

Luis tightened his grip on the shovel and prepared for whatever was coming next. If he had to fight Mike or even kill him, he would not hesitate. Luis was happy to realize that his buddy, Jerry, was finally coming around to see that Mike might not be telling the complete truth about the job and was even questioning Mike out loud. Hopefully, Jerry's revelation wasn't too late.

Mike looked back at the two pathetic excuses for men, cowering back by the dried-up pond. That was exactly what he figured they would do. So predictable, he thought. Mike reached up to grab one of the iron rings on the gate; the shimmering light moved away as he touched it. He tugged on the ring, but the door did not budge. Mike attempted again with two hands this time pulling with all his might. A deep grunt escaped his lips and then he stumbled back; the door still did not budge.

"Stuck, huh? Come on Army man, use your muscles," taunted Jerry, feeling more confident teasing Mike since Luis had just done it.

Luis grinned at Jerry. Attaboy, he thought. Jerry was growing some balls—finally.

Mike did not verbally attack either of them or express any anger. "Well, it looks like I need your help to open these doors. Please, could you step up and assist me? Please?"

Jerry proudly straightened up and stepped towards the gate to assist Mike. His foot twisted as his weight crushed something beneath the layer of dust. Suddenly a loud crack rang out, and he looked down at his foot just as a half-demolished human skull rolled aside and stared back at him.

Instinctively, Jerry jumped back losing his balance and tripped into the small empty pond. Trying to break his fall, he reached out to the dead tree which stood forlornly in the middle. Grabbing a large branch, he screamed as its prickly thorns easily poked through his hand like a pin cushion.

"What the fuck!" he exclaimed. Blood from his hand dripped down the branch and into the pond.

"Luis, help the baby before he cries for his mommy," mocked Mike.

Jerry witnessed a new expression on Mike's face which he had never seen before. Luis recognized it immediately that it was pure wickedness. The sight terrified him, and he tried to hide his emotional reaction from Mike. Run. That is exactly what he wanted to do. Escape, but not without Jerry.

He tightened his grip on the shovel and cautiously approached Jerry. He kept one eye on Mike and readied himself to use the shovel as a weapon if needed. His movement stirred up the dust which covered most of the debris and prevented him from identifying what exactly he was crushing underfoot. He reached Jerry safely. Luis began to pull Jerry's hand off the branch, but hesitated when he saw that a blanket of tinier needle-like thorns had fully penetrated Jerry's hand.

"I'm sorry man. If I pull your hand off, those thorns will tear it apart." Luis' voice crackled with emotion.

Abruptly, a tree branch swung around and embedded itself into the back of Luis' thigh. Both men cried out in agony as the dead tree came to life and, with branches, like tentacles, wrapped its thorny appendages around them both. The tree was growing taller and taller lifting them off the ground and turned them upside down. Long, needle-like thorns penetrated their bodies causing their blood to trickle into the shallow pond beneath them.

"Mike!" whimpered Jerry.

"Help us!" bellowed Luis as he struggled to free himself.

The sinister grin remained on Mike's face.

Both men struggled. Their screams intensified with the realization that Mike would not help them.

Branches slithered towards their faces and abruptly crammed deep into their mouths. Screams switched to gurgling as blood streamed out their nose and ears.

Mike watched his companions' bodies shrivel up as the last of their blood drained into the pond. Their withered remains were then tossed aside, landing with a resounding thump. The thick layer of dust quickly folded over the corpses as they blended in with the other skeletal remains that filled the room. The sacrifice tree shrank back to its miniature size, lying in wait for its next victim.

Mike had stood motionless on the steps to the Gate the entire time as he watched his companions struggle to their deaths. How's it feel? he thought as their last breaths were screams. He watched without emotion as their lives slowly shriveled away, waiting for the satisfying feeling of revenge to engulf him. He fantasized about their painful demise day after day, hour after hour, and finally it had come to be passed. He waited for it, waited for the satisfaction to fill his heart as payment for their abandoning him to die in the desert. Unfortunately, that satisfaction never came; not even a morsel of gratification filled his heart. The emptiness that consumed him continued to exist and his hunger to kill only grew stronger.

On the edge of the shallow pond closest to the Gate, a swirling wind blew clear the debris. The floor had the same smooth marble as the walls, and a small chiseled groove led from the pond to the Gate. Most might assume that liquid would flow down from the Gate and into the pond, but not in this case. Mike watched as the blood trickled out of the pond and along the groove, then crawled up, yes, up into the carvings of the Gate. As soon as the blood touched the doors, the glowing emerald energy retreated from the area where the blood and wood met. The light faded completely from the Gate. The illuminating energy now hovered only over the symbols that lined both of its sides. The pond was completely empty of blood now. as all of it had climbed up to fill the carvings in the Gate's doors.

The room vibrated as the impenetrable doors of the great Gate scraped open. It didn't stop shaking until the Gate opened completely. Torches which lined the walls of the chamber sparked to life fully illuminating the area. Mike approached this portal to another world but saw nothing. It only revealed a black void devouring all light that attempted to penetrate its realm.

The chamber fully aglow now revealed the true nature of the debris scattered about. It was human ashes, not dust, and there were bone fragments littered around the pond and Sacrifice Tree. The dusty, decayed remains of these bodies gave the illusion of a smooth gray surface and concealed the layers of evil carnage.

"Samael? Samael, are you there? Please tell me you are. I want this nightmare to end," Mike's voice was that of a little boy—quiet and weak. His eyes searched the void but saw nothing. His voice quivered as he attempted to speak again, but this time nothing escaped his mouth. His confidence gone. He was now a lost child searching for the security of a parent's voice, telling him he would be safe and there was nothing to fear. The void beyond the Gate failed to provide him the reassurance he sought.

A faint animal grunt rose from deep in the darkness. Its snarling tones and low pitch changed from that of a wild beast to a clear commanding male voice. "Nightmare? That's what you call it, Michael? A Nightmare?"

"Samael!"

"Yes, Michael. It is I. You insult me! Telling me that answering a dying man's cries, who was pleading for his life so he can see his soulmate once more has been a nightmare? How ungrateful! I only asked in return—my freedom from this prison." Mike saw no physical form yet. He could only hear the voice resonating from the void.

Mike stood rooted directly in front of the gate with his head hung down in shame in response to Samael's words. Drained of any confidence, his body trembled, then he sobbed.

The outline of a large horned figure, about a foot shorter than the height of the Gate, approached. The shape shrunk down to about seven feet and morphed into a humanoid form. Samael burst out of the darkness, stopping a few feet from Mike on the opposite side of the gate. Samael, towering over Mike, was regal-looking with raven black hair touched by gray at the temples. Two small horns protruded just slightly from his forehead. A threatening confidence and power emanated from Samael causing Mike to take a step back.

"I just want my life back. Like you promised," pleaded Mike. "I freed you! Now free me like we agreed so my fiancée and I can move on with our lives."

Samael grinned fiendishly as he attempted to walk through the gate. The shimmering emerald light from the symbols on the wall lashed out at him, exploding into a ball of energy and catapulting Samael back into the darkness. A foul, ear-piercing scream echoed across the room, causing Mike to drop to the floor and cover his ears. Then silence for a long time. Or, at least to Mike it felt like a long time.

"You haven't completed your task, Michael. You failed me." Samael's irritated tone changed to a calm authoritative one as he emerged from the darkness again. He stood at the threshold, inspecting the Gate thoroughly. "You've only succeeded in opening the Gate. The Dragon Spirit is still present and strong enough to keep the portal between our worlds closed. You didn't use enough innocent blood!"

That word, blood, rippled through Mike's thoughts. He had seen more than his share of it while fighting in the Middle East and had just now witnessed his comrades drained of it. The unending nightmares of innocent women and children scattered in the streets, bleeding to death, continued to haunt him. His dreams intertwined with his memories of staggering through the desert, covered in his own blood. The intermingled images flashed before his eyes causing him to whimper softly. In his nightmares, no matter how many women and children he attempted to save, or was it to kill them? Either way—they all died. He couldn't recall which it was anymore. "More Blood? But you said..." He stood up to face Samael again.

"You're questioning me?"

Mike dropped to the ground again. But this time it was not Mike's weakness, but the power from Samael's own voice which forced him to kneel. Mike could not resist his evil powers. His wounds from the blast that had nearly killed him in the desert reappeared. He bled again. Some of his organs slipped out of his wounds.

"Even though I cannot pass into your world, my powers can still reach you and easily take my gift of life from you. I see you need to be reminded of that pact we agreed upon. I said we need more innocent blood. Do you understand?"

The pain was so intense that Mike could not verbally respond to Samael's question, so he just shook his head in agreement. The hold on him finally eased up and his wounds disappeared again. "So, you're going to drain my blood and kill me? Go ahead just kill me." He remained kneeling.

Samael's thundering roar echoed throughout the stone chamber. "I said innocent blood, my boy. You do not have a drop in your body anymore. You lost it when you killed all those women and children. Or have you forgotten? You mowed them down without a second thought. They weren't a threat; they didn't even have weapons. Yet, you still shot them because you enjoyed watching the blood pump out of their bodies. You claimed it was to keep the world safe, yet what harm could they truly have done to you? Is it out of fear that you kill, or is it really for the pleasure of it? Hmm?"

"Stop! Stop it! That's not true!" yelled Mike as he stood up and faced Samael straight on.

"Now, there's the Goliath I remember helping. Glad to have you back, my son." Samael paced back and forth on the other side of the Gate. "Let me consider our options."

From the other end of the massive chamber, the glow from the illuminating moss slowly died away. Then it began falling off the ceiling and walls in clumps, splattering down onto the granite floor. As the moss piled on top of itself, it merged and formed gooey, fleshy blobs of various sizes. Dozens of them appeared. The blobs transformed into

Lemures, the lowest creature-caste in Hell. They lacked intelligence, so they existed as slaves to the fallen angels; imprisoned together. A Lemure's loyalty to its master was only as strong as whoever was the most powerful in their vicinity. They had caused many tragic events throughout history with their ability to easily slip through minuscule cracks between both worlds and possess living creatures or inanimate objects. Chaos prevailed wherever these hideous horrors appeared in our world.

"My children, you still live! I thought the Dragon Spirit destroyed you all. But now I see the foul creature only imprisoned you." Samael's evil grin grew as he recalculated his plans.

"Children?" questioned Mike as he watched the gelatinous blobs of veiny flesh crawl towards him.

"Michael, you might be released from our contract sooner than you thought. My Lemures can help you break open the portal by bringing more innocent blood to the Tree of Sacrifice."

"Why do you need me at all then? Why not just have them do it?"

Samael chuckled as he assessed the naivete of the human who stood before him. "They are not high on the intelligence chart and their attention span is less than..." He searched for just the right comparison. "...less than a three-year-old. I need you to keep them focused on our goal—returning with innocent blood."

"Help them? With what?"

"To find their way up to the surface. I can guide them back here, but I need you to lead them out of here."

"How many people are we talking about?"

"Hmm. Good question." Samael thought about that as he paced back and forth along the edge of the portal. "A half dozen or so virgins? That would annihilate the dragon's spiritual lock on the Gate. Know of any nearby?"

"You knew from the beginning those two idiots wouldn't be enough to open the portal, didn't you? You lied to me."

"Bent the truth a little, perhaps. Besides, you wanted to kill them anyway. I figured one of them had to be a virgin, such weak pathetic souls. One would expect a bit more kick from their blood to do more damage. Guess I miscalculated."

Mike stepped towards Samael as both were now only a few inches apart; only the glowing emerald barrier shimmered between them. He stared intensely at Samael while puffing out his chest to intimidate him. "I should just fucking leave right now and you figure it out yourself."

The Lemures made their way across the chamber floor, stopping next to Mike. The blobs melted into one another and morphed into a large single creature. Their veins pumped black blood through their translucent bodies. Their mouths contained needle-like teeth, like the Sacrifice Tree's thorns, protruding whenever they opened their mouths. They continued to merge into one another and finally transformed into a large human-like form. The single gelatinous Lemure mimicked Mike's gestures and movements.

"So, we're needing six virgins? Really? Anything else I should know? Blonde? Brunette? You realize this is San Francisco, right?" Mike said sarcastically.

"Yes, yes, I know exactly where this Gate opens up. I've been here before. Virgin blood destroys the Dragon Spirit's essence, but blood from several souls with some kind of innocence should do just as well. It's the mere substance of their innocence that weakens the Dragon Spirit. The purer the blood, the less we will need. My Lemures will bring them back here and place the bodies on the Sacrifice Tree, so their blood will fill the pond." Samael said, ignoring Mike and watching in amusement, like a proud parent watching their child walk for the first time, as the newly created man-creature imitated Mike's movement. It then lost its balance and fell to the floor. Several of the Lemures disconnected from the single form.

The Lemures separated into smaller units again. Samael stared intensely back at Mike as fire reflected in his eyes momentarily. "You just need to lead my children to the surface, and they will find the people. Simple enough? Even your dead comrades could handle a simple request like that. Can you?"

"So, they will just follow me?" Mike asked as he watched them surround him like little puppies, jumping with excitement for their first walk. Suddenly, they pounced on him all at once and slipped under his clothes, then traveled up his legs.

"Actually," smirked Samael. "They will travel in you. They can easily possess any living creature, but it might be a little uncomfortable for you at first."

Mike screamed in agony as the fleshy forms entered his body through his mouth, ears, eyes, and nose. They entered through all of his orifices.

"Or, it might be insufferable. I don't really know."

Mike's body convulsed as the Lemures penetrated his body. He dropped to his knees, then fell over onto his side and curled into a fetal position. The remaining creatures circled his body as they looked for a passageway in.

CHAPTER 4

The Shift Begins

The Tony's Food Mart sign was no longer a crisp glowing neon beacon, but a washed-out, paint-peeling sign in the morning light. The U.S. Mint building remained perched on the hill behind the store. The parking lot was bustling with vehicles coming and going while customers scurried in and out of the store.

A gray-primer colored 1977 Datsun 280z zipped into the parking lot, dodging several customers. It cut off a van and stole the parking slot the van had been waiting for from the opposite direction. The lady in the van slammed on her brakes and stopped just in time to avoid hitting the Datsun. She honked twice, then drove further down the row, searching for another parking space. As the Datsun's engine turned off, several puffs of black smoke sputtered out of its exhaust. The engine backfired at the last moment before shutting down.

The driver's door swung open, gouging a deep scratch into a white Mercedes parked in the next space.

Alan popped out of the driver's side. He was dressed in the traditional assistant manager uniform: pressed black slacks, ironed white cotton button-up dress shirt, and steel-enforced-toe black dress shoes. He was lanky. His height made him look like a man, but his boyish face betrayed his youthful age of early twenties. He bent down and checked out his reflection in the driver's window, then pulled out a Tony's Food Mart employee badge, attaching it to his shirt pocket. Next, he pulled out a clip-on tie from his pocket and secured it onto his shirt collar. Finally, satisfied with how he looked, Alan headed towards the store.

He was barely a foot from his car when a cart from out of nowhere ran into his backside, almost knocking him over. "Hey, what the fuck!"

"Oh sorry, Honey. Did I hurt you?" innocently asked Mrs. Murphy, who was dressed in a modest yellow sun dress, white gloves, and a hat which coordinated with her outfit. "Are you sure you're okay?" again asked the sweetest little old lady anyone had ever encountered, while she nonchalantly reached one of her hands around Alan's waist and caressed his butt; not quite where the cart hit him though.

Alan responded at the first moment he felt her hand squeezing his butt cheek and jumped away from her.

"Hey! Stop that! Yes, I'm fine. Really, I'm fine. Mrs. Murphy, you can't run into people just to molest them."

"Young people have such dirty minds nowadays!" She threw her nose up in the air and walked away. She scampered off while hitting the corner of his car as she left.

"Or, hit their cars either!" yelled Alan.

She flipped him off with her petite middle finger while she continued bumping into cars and people as she wandered off through the parking lot.

Alan began his trek towards the front entrance of the store again. He smiled at the customers as he passed them. He made eye contact with them and return his typical canned smile which he had been doing for over the last five years of working at this store.

He alternated between his standard, "How are you doing today?" or "Did you find everything you were looking for?" statements, though he did not really care what the customers' responses were. He didn't want to put too much effort into the light exchange of words, otherwise the customer would want to have a deep conversation about themselves. He knew most of the longtime customers' life stories and their shopping habits. He knew more information about their personal lives than probably their own families, since most customers loved talking about themselves. They rarely asked Alan about his own life or what he was doing for the holidays or weekends. He was fine with not talking about his personal life as there wasn't really much to talk about since he did nothing other than work. The customers were always ready to tell him all about what they were doing, and he trained himself to act like he was interested.

He started working at this grocery store on his sixteenth birthday as a bagger. His father informed him from a very young age that when he turned sixteen that he would have to work if he wanted anything from that point on. His father had no intentions of supporting him since his alcohol habit was more important than spending money on his son. So Alan ran away and lived on the streets at age fifteen. After a few days, though, he found himself tired and starving. He walked into a small corner store to steal whatever food he could slide into his jacket, but the shop owner caught him. The owner did not call the police but sat him down and offered him some hot chocolate. They talked a bit about why Alan wanted the food. Alan didn't want to say anything to the man at first, but something broke inside Alan, like a ruptured dam, and his life story about his father and running away poured out of his mouth.

As Alan finished his story, the owner's response was just "Humm?". He stood up and looked down at Alan and offered him a job—to clean the floors and stock the shelves. In return, he could stay in the back room at night and off the streets. The shop owner would even bring food down to Alan, but he had to promise to finish high school so he could make something of himself and not waste his life. The owner lived above the store with his niece who had special needs. There was a side entrance to the store to which Alan was given a key so he could come and go on his own. Alan accepted the agreement. He worked very hard both at the shop and at school.

It was about a year later that the owner's niece passed away and abruptly announced that he was leaving the city for a long overdue vacation. He told Alan that he could move into the upstairs apartment since he wasn't sure when he was coming back and wanted to make it looked like someone still lived there, even though the store was closed. The owner even helped Alan get a job at Tony's Food Mart so that he'd have money to buy food.

The store was a safe place away from his father. Alan never looked back and never regretted his decision to escape his father's physical abuse. He had not spoken with his father since the day he ran away with just the clothes he was wearing and a small backpack of what little food he could find in the house. He had seen his father occasionally on the Muni train system, but easily avoided him since his father was usually drunk and unaware of his surroundings.

Shortly after Alan turned eighteen, he graduated from high school and was also promoted to a checker position. He learned about the functions of all the store's departments. Now at twenty-two, he was about to enter the store as an assistant manager. He was excited to start his first day in this new position because he now had the title for what he had been doing for the last year, though it had been without the title or the salary.

The store manager, Mr. Helovich, was happy Alan always stepped up and filled in so eagerly around the store, but even happier not having to pay him the assistant manager's salary. That was until the Union stepped in and pointed out to Mr. Helovich that he violated the Union contract. They would fine the store if he did not promote Alan to the proper position and pay scale for the level of work he was performing. One thing Mr. Helovich hated more than people stealing from him and his store was having to pay anything to the Union, since he felt they interfered with how he really wanted to manage his store.

Alan had completed the two weeks of training offered at the corporate office last week and was returning to the store today as the official Assistant Manager. Part of him wanted to go find his father and show him what a noble life he had made for himself, but he was afraid his father would show up at the store and embarrass him or cause him to lose his job. He would not risk that. In a sense, he became the man his father wanted him to be—a practical, no risk kind of guy who focused on staying secure in his world, reducing any chance to cause him to end up broke and homeless on the street. That was something Alan would never risk happening to him again. His promotion confirmed to him that his decision to skip college and keep working hard had paid off.

He knew everything about the store. It was comfortable, safe, and predictable. He made enough money to pay what little bills he had. Well, at least that is what he kept telling himself. The world's uncertainty bothered him, but the grocery life was one where he knew what to expect each day and it was controllable most days. This store was his home, or better stated, it was his security blanket and he saw no reason or desire to leave it.

"Excuse me, Sir? Excuse me, you dropped something?" asked Ms. Pepper. Her loud, lime green and white pantsuit, along with her matching lime green and white streaked hairdo showed she was either one confident cougar or a lunatic on the prowl.

Alan looked behind him and saw nothing on the ground. Before he could ask her what he had dropped, Ms. Pepper informed him, "You dropped your footsteps. You better go back and pick them up." She roared with laughter and walked off, targeting her next victim with her jokes.

She was a long-time customer at the store. She was shopping there long before Alan worked there. Her jokes were different every time he encountered her, which was almost a daily basis. Alan was waiting for the day she repeated a joke, so he could respond with the correct answer before she did. But in all those years, she never repeated a joke.

As time passed, Alan became curious and asked the other employees what they knew about her. They told him a couple of different stories, but the common thread of gossip was that she was a powerhouse executive many years ago with little sense of humor. Supposedly, her husband told her that her wardrobe lacked zest and flare and her self-centered conversations bored everyone. He informed her that he felt more emotional support from her brother than from her. Needless to say,

Ms. Pepper's husband ended up leaving with her own brother. Shortly after that, she had a nervous breakdown and disappeared for several months. Then out of the blue, she showed up one day shopping at the store again and dressed in an outlandish colored pantsuit and a hairdo that matched to the craziness of her outfit. This became a normal choice of attire with multiple color combinations. She talked to whoever gave her a moment of their time and attention. She always opened the conversation with a joke. She laughed immediately after delivering the punchline, then jetted off before the person could respond.

The front lobby was calm compared to all the customers in the parking lot. Only a couple of shoppers were being checked out. A woman in sweats, curlers covered by a headscarf, and sunglasses stood next to the news rack. She was deeply engrossed reading about the latest gossip from Hollywood. Alan wondered why she would not just buy the magazine and take it home. She was there every morning reading through several magazines. He did not know her name since she never went through his line when he was checking. In fact, he didn't recall ever seeing her go through a register line. She would just be by the magazines and then disappeared after an hour or so.

Two registers were open. The express lane for 10 items or less, and a regular lane. The checker,

Mandy, was working the express lane and had two customers waiting in line. She carefully examined each item the customer was purchasing. She looked at each one closely, then stared at the customer and smiled or frowned at them, depending on if it was a healthy choice or not.

"Really? A dozen donuts, Mr. Greyson? Oh, and a soda, too, for lunch! No big surprise here. How many times have I told you that you're destroying your organs? And yet, every day you come in and continue to buy this crap. Again, and again. You're killing yourself. I'm telling you. When will you realize that?" She ended her rant and just stared at the seventy-year-old man waiting for his response. "Huh?"

The customer looked down at his items and truly did not appear to be disturbed by her comments at all. He wore an obnoxious over-sized Hawaiian shirt and tight, bright blue spandex bicycle shorts, which revealed an unusually large bulge protruding from his groin.

"I know, but I love your daily verbal abuse. Why else would I be here every day? It reminds me of my late wife, actually wives. You can abuse me anytime you like. So, when are you going to let me take you out for dinner, Sweetie?" Mr. Greyson requested while his caterpillar eyebrows rose up and down several times, as if attempting to hypnotize her into saying yes.

"Maybe when you start eating healthier, like some vegetables at least. And, when I decide I'm into guys over a hundred years old. $10.84, please. Oh, and I included the cucumber in your shorts. Not impressed, Mr. Greyson. Not at all. Sorry."

"See, I got a vegetable after all. That's healthy. I'll be back later today and see if you've changed your mind, Sweetie." He handed her a twenty-dollar bill, then grabbed his bag and walked towards the exit without waiting for his change.

"Technically, the cucumber is a fruit. Like you," she responded, but he was already out the door. The next customer stepped up and placed her over-stuffed coupon organizer on the counter and began pulling out various coupons while some spilled out and onto the floor. Mandy started her routine of inspecting each item and then assessing the customer if it was a healthy choice or not. As Alan passed the Express register, Mandy smiled and winked at him. Then, she returned to her close examination of her customer's purchases.

At the regular register, Paul was finishing up on a large order which completely buried his counter with groceries. No bagger was around to assist. The female customer appeared to be in no rush from what Alan observed as she flirted with Paul like all female customers did when they laid eyes on him. Paul picked up the phone and used the overhead paging system to call for a bagger to help.

He started bagging her groceries, but she kept pulling his attention away as she asked him irrelevant questions while leaning over the counter with her low-cut blouse, jiggling her breasts.

Paul did not acknowledge her like she was hoping as he bent over to place a bag on the bottom of the cart. She then practically climbed over the counter to get a good look at his firm round ass in his tight pants.

Paul stood back up and noticed Alan passing by. They exchanged the typical "guy nod" to each other and he returned to bagging. They did not really need to say much more since they were roommates. Alan was jealous of his roommate's charisma, actually unbelievably jealous.

Paul had the typical athletic football build since he played college football and worked out on the field or in the gym almost daily. One more year at San Francisco State University and then Paul's father was having him transfer somewhere back East to a more prestigious university, hoping a scout would spot him and sign him onto a Pro team.

Unfortunately, Paul was the typical dumb jock that every woman wanted to sleep with, while every guy hated him because of that, but secretly wished they could be just like him.

Alan struggled to understand how Paul had such a happy-go-lucky attitude. He wondered if Paul was even aware of the power and control he held over women just by using his dimpled-smile, exposing the gleam of his perfect white teeth. He made them weak in the knees with his looks and could talk them into doing anything for him. Alan wished he had that type of power over women, since most woman only saw him as a friend or a brother, never a lover.

It was Paul's abilities that Alan admired that convinced him to agree to be roommates. They had only been roommates for a couple of months now, and still no luck in his charm, rubbing off on Alan or catching any of his female rejects.

Paul agreed to be roommates because the Dorms were interfering with his football training, as he immediately discovered that the college girls were offering sex every time he got back to his room. He'd been late to practice numerous times and was about to get kicked off the team.

That action immediately grabbed the attention of Paul's father, who was one of the many Vice Presidents of Tony's Food Mart corporation. He placed his son in this store as a Checker to keep his mind off the girls and out of trouble. His other objective was to get his son to experience a blue-collar job so the hard work would motivate Paul to focus on his football career and not get distracted.

Between attending school and working at the store, Paul's father decided it would be best to find

Paul a convenient and safe place to live in The City. His son would be close to the university to attend both his practices and classes and not spend hours stuck in traffic trying to return home to Marin county. His father discussed his son's needs with Mr. Helovich. They both approached Alan and told him that he was going to be Paul's roommate. So it really wasn't a choice. When your store manager and Vice-President approach you in that manner, there isn't much to discuss and definitely no possibility to say no.

Alan had thought about it only for a few seconds as they offered it to him with free room and board. The catch, he just needed to make sure Paul showed up on time for practice, classes, and work. To date, that agreement had been easy to maintain.

As the time came to move in with Paul, Alan was not thrilled about the change since it really was not his choice. He had not thought it through when he accepted the offer and was actually scared of this big change since he had been on his own for over six years now. Alan was still in the place that the shop owner had offered to him while he went on an extended vacation. Six years later, the shop owner still had not returned. No letters or indication of when he would be back.

Once Alan found out that the apartment with Paul was located in the Marina District, he forced himself to push through his fears since he had dreamt of living there one day. He knew he would never earn enough money to live there on his own. Besides, he thought, he could always go back to his old apartment if it didn't work out. The thought of catching one or two of Paul's rejected girlfriends also heavily motivated him to get past that uneasy feeling of the unknown.

So far, he could not snag any of the female leftovers even though there was one almost every other day. All they would do is call Alan and ask if Paul was available or they would ask him to pass a message on to Paul since Paul wouldn't return their calls or text messages. They saw Alan more as Paul's receptionist since once Paul got what he wanted from them, he ceased contact. He would quickly move on to his next conquest within the San Francisco female population.

Paul enjoyed having Alan as a roommate, at least that is what Alan thought, since Paul could show off his trophies each morning to Alan. Paul played it well. He neglected to mention to his female guests that he had a roommate and the setup was done. The two guys had made a deal that Alan would get rid of the girls in the morning so Paul could leave early for football practice or school. As soon as he was gone, Alan played loud music and made a lot of noise in the kitchen which would usually startle the girl awake. She would then realize Paul was gone, have an outburst of frustration, grab her stuff, and leave. Paul didn't see it as mistreatment but believed his female friends wanted to make him happy and sex made him happy.

Occasionally, a half-naked woman, hearing the shower running, would stumble into the kitchen and make breakfast for Paul, unaware that he had already left the apartment. Alan would come out of the bathroom in a towel and just sit down. They always left immediately at that point; though Alan had hoped something more would happen but it never did.

The female customer that Paul was waiting on continued flirting with him. He was just about finished bagging her groceries.

"I'm here, I'm here," announced Peli as she rushed up to Paul's register. She pulled out a couple of large paper bags and started bagging what little groceries remained. Peli never looked at the female customer, but just talked to Paul directly. Another one charmed. "I was late dropping off Lily at daycare. Then the Muni train broke down. Can you imagine that? It always happens on the days I work early. Then I..."

The whining continued. Alan just tuned it out since that was all Peli ever did was to talk and talk about nothing but herself. But, once you got past the half-shaved head, the remaining hair ratted out, tattoos around the neck, and the bullring in her nose, she actually was an exquisite young woman. He wondered if she was like that before she had Lily or if the transformation occurred after giving birth. Alan was confident that no guy would have dared approach her in her present state, let alone have sex with her. She looked like she would rip his member right off and devour it. He had a sudden flash of what her daughter possibly looked like- a princess dress with half her hair shaved off while holding a switchblade instead of a royal scepter.

For a moment, Alan chuckled at the image lingering in his mind but was snapped back into reality as he felt the frigid stare directed at him from an ancient, stone-faced Asian lady just a couple of registers past Paul. Her eyes pierced his corneas and reached down his throat, trying to steal his soul. She always made him speechless, as she could break through any walls of protection you prepared before engaging in conversation with her.

Alan had no clue how old she was, but knew she was the oldest clerk in the store. Some coworkers joked about her being here before the store opened and they just built it around her. Her black polyester, conservative pantsuit and her gray-hair pulled back in a snug bun did not help soften her appearance. From what Alan observed over the years working at the store, she was someone that no one really talked to unless it was work related. They were afraid to converse with her and avoided her whenever possible. That was easy to accomplish since she was the front booth clerk and usually in the booth handling customer issues, or setting up cash drawers for the day, or removing cash from the drawers throughout the day, and then updating the sales reports from the previous day. She was pretty much stuck in the booth.

Alan rarely saw her out on the floor. So, he took it upon himself to step out, challenging himself to be friendly towards her when an opportunity opened up, even though it scared the shit out of him to do it. He wanted everyone to like him and was going to do whatever he could to be on her good side. He made the effort to talk with her just to see if he could get her to smile. But, after the last several years of trying, he still was unsuccessful. In fact, over the years, the conversations usually turned out to be more like a sword fight with words, and he never won. In the beginning, she only grunted at him. In time, she actually used real words which cut deep into Alan. He constantly wondered if she insulted him on purpose or was it just a defense mechanism to keep people away. At present, his relationship with her was at first an attempt to be nice, but after that, if she insulted him, which she usually did, he would attack back. Alan did not like doing that to her since she was an old lady and he wanted to show her respect. So, when it came to her, a first attempt was as much as he would give.

"Good Morning, Grace," he said grinning with the friendliest smile he could muster, with the hope that this might be the day she would say something nice back to him. Maybe she would congratulate him on his promotion, perhaps.

"Mr. Tony's Food Mart, himself. Welcome back to the real world." She called out as she switched out a register tray, then picked up a stack of five trays and carried them with one arm like a waitress carrying dirty plates.

For such a petite old lady, she had some unusually powerful arms, he thought. "Grace, come on. Alan, just Alan. I thought you'd be happy I'm back?"

"The brown-nose kiss-up leaves for two weeks of management training and he returns as Mr. Just Alan. Nice. The employees will surely respect you now. Oh. Wait. They never respected you before, why would they now?

Annoyed by that comment, Alan's buttons were strategically pushed and his reaction was to attack her back. It was part of a conversation he had heard a young slimy sleazeball say to her when he tried to cash a check at the front booth with no ID. Grace refused to cash it per store policy and said the customer needed to present some form of ID. He started swearing at her but her expression remained calm and unchanged. But then, he made the fatal comment which had him wake up on the ground several minutes later with the police standing over him. That was the first time anyone saw Grace lose control. She had dropped him to the ground with one solid punch to the jaw. Mr. Helovich was angry with her and told her that if she ever struck another customer in the store, he would fire her. Against Alan's better judgement, he was going to slam her and launch the A-bomb as he poised himself to run like hell, if needed.

"Yes, Mamasan." Alan watched closely as Grace raised her right eyebrow and her eyes locked onto him. He wanted to take it back. He wanted to run to the back of the store and hide. It was too late as he had pushed the button which unleashed god-knows-what and Alan did not want to know *what*. Suddenly his mouth opened, and he blurted out something he did not even expect. "I am the Assistant Manager now and your boss. I am warning you I can fire you for insubordination." He tried to sound as confident as possible which was tough since she scared him more than Mr. Helovich, who was the scariest guy Alan had ever met.

Grace raised her other eyebrow and a small grin emerged on her face. "Well, Mr. Helovich, your boss, has been calling you to his office for the past hour. I think you're the one who's being insubordinate. Don't forget he can fire you." The grin grew into a full smile showing her perfect pearly white teeth. She had won that round and knew it. She did not linger to gloat over her victory, as she turned and was about to disappear with several cash drawers into the front booth.

"Thank you, most gracious Mamasan." He slowly bowed filled with relief as she began to disappear from his sight; retaliation avoided.

Alan's comment stopped Grace dead in her tracks. She stepped backwards from the doorway and turned towards him. She held her head high and confident. "I'm Dutch! Your brainless profiling is childish. And by the way, I speak proper English unlike you. You are such a pathetic social leech." This time she slipped into the booth before Alan could respond, which was easy to do since he stood there racking his brain to decipher what she had just said.

Alan stood there for a couple of seconds pondering her statement. He wondered what a 'pathetic social leech' was, and if he truly was one? Damn, she did it to me again, he thought. One day I will win one of our verbal battles. Even though he would not admit it to anyone, he was starting to enjoy these challenging encounters. There was something exciting about it.

Alan walked back passed the Express register. There were no more customers in line, so Mandy stood there staring at him while batting her eyes. Alan reluctantly returned a half-smile as he approached and was still processing his last conversation with Grace in his head.

She sprung out of the register and gave him a big hug. "Welcome back! Don't listen to her. She's probably been sucking on sour grapefruit all morning." She continued fluttering her eyes at him. "Mr. Helovich has been screaming at everyone ever since you left."

"More than his usual temper tantrums?"

She nodded yes.

"Thanks for the heads up."

Alan left the checkout area and approached the Produce Department. At first glance, the produce wet racks and tables appeared to be setup perfectly for the morning shoppers, but he knew from years of experience working in this department, and from his recent training, that what looks good on the surface may have rotten fruit or vegetables just a layer or two below. Slimy lettuce could be hidden underneath if it hasn't been rotated properly. When he worked produce and was short on time he just threw the new stuff on top, straightened it up, and it would look fresh again. Now as an assistant manager, he was going to have to break that practice and enforce the correct policy with the other produce workers.

The two front promotional tables were fully stocked. The first table was full of natural beige-colored pistachios, while the other one was hand-stacked with colossal artichokes built up into the form of a Mayan pyramid—flat on top.

Just then a juvenile delinquent wearing skate shoes rolled over to the pistachio table and scooped up some nuts. He popped off the shells and tossed the nuts into his mouth. He picked up another handful and ate some but when he saw Alan approaching, he spit the nuts back onto the table.

"Hey, you need to pay for that. You can't just stand there and eat them."

"I'm sampling them!" He spit more nuts back onto the table then he held his hand out and dropped the remaining nuts on the floor in front of Alan. "Whatcha gonna do 'bout it?"

Alan wanted to throw him over the table but knew he would lose his job if he did that. He went to grab the kid's t-shirt, but a customer came around the corner and into sight, so he flattened his hand out and just patted the kid on the shoulder. "You need to pay for what you ate."

"Fuck you, Mister," he pushed Alan's hand off his shoulder. "Whatcha gonna do 'bout it?" He skated up to the front lobby, turned around, and stuck out his long, pierced tongue at Alan. Then while sticking up both middle fingers he rolled out the front door, backwards.

Echoing throughout the entire store from the overhead paging system, Mr. Helovich's voice boomed down. This voice all employees knew and immediately stopped everything to listen to carefully, since he rarely used the paging system unless it was an emergency. "MR. CHERRY, PLEASE REPORT TO MY OFFICE...NOW!"

Alan looked up at the one-way glass which lined the top of the wall to the ceiling on the far side of the Produce Department. The store manager's office was situated upstairs and allowed him to view the entire store from that location. With the one-way glass, no one could tell if anyone was in the office watching you or not.

"YES NOW, MR. CHERRY!",

Yep, he was being watched for sure with that response. Alan looked away from the one-way mirrors because even though he could not see Mr. Helovich, Alan felt his eyes burning into him. He held back a little from moving too quickly towards the back room as he hoped to calm his boss' fury. Since Alan was an assistant manager now, he should have some kind of management pull with his own boss. At least, he hoped he did.

Alan's attention shifted down from the ceiling and along the back wall of the Produce Department where his eyes glimpsed Missy standing next to the produce door which led into the backroom. She was struggling with a rolling rack of beauty supplies as she attempted to push it through the swinging doors. Various boxes kept slipping off the rack and onto the floor as she attempted to catch them before they hit the ground.

Amused by the juggling act, Alan thought this was his chance to jump in to help her and be the knight in shining armor and save her day. He also wanted to find out what happened on their date as it ended awkwardly. He wanted to, no, he needed to clear the air between them. He was unable to talk to her while he was away at management training and since returning. She hadn't answered any of his calls or replied to any of his text messages.

Missy's appearance was that of a mannequin: immaculate makeup, tiny waist, long legs. Her non-natural blonde and highly stylized hair was not a quick wash and wear style but took hours to achieve. She had even altered her uniform to compliment her skinny waist and added a loose colorful scarf around her neck. She stood out from the other female store clerks.

She noticed Alan approaching. Sheer panic reflected on her face. She threw the fallen lipstick randomly into the rolling cart, positioning herself so the cart was between her and Alan. Then, she pulled as hard as possible to get the cart through the swinging doors. She disappeared into the back room while several lipsticks fell onto the produce floor. She didn't stop to pick them up.

CHAPTER 5

Pecking Order

The backroom was small and only able to handle a few grocery pallets lined up along one side of the wall. The merchandise on these pallets were the sale items for the week which needed to be grabbed quickly to restock the shelves throughout the day. On the opposite side of the wall were three metal doors: One led into the dairy box, another into the freezer box, and the last one was the door to the meat cooler. This back area had a short set of stairs that went up to the loading dock staging area. Another set of stairs led down into the basement, next to the small freight elevator, and there was yet another set of stairs that headed up and made a "T" to the manager's office and the employee's breakroom.

The larger elevator could handle the weight of three milk pallets. Each floor needed a motorized pallet mover since an employee could not fit in the elevator if three pallets were placed in it at the same time.

The smaller freight elevator was located next to the produce double doors which led out to the store floor. The produce clerks used this elevator to bring up trimmed lettuces and various items to refill the wet rack and the hard tables throughout the day. They regularly used a pallet mover to easily move the product on to the floor.

Missy burst through the swinging produce doors pulling a standing rack which was full of various general merchandise. She reached for the small elevator's down button and frantically pushed it several times while looking back at the produce doors. Frustrated, she pushed it several times again. She heard the elevator hydraulics moan as the elevator rose from the basement to greet her. She leaned forward and looked through the small window on the floor door to see how much longer until it would reach her floor. It travels so slowly, she thought, as she was desperately trying to get away and disappear before Alan caught up with her. He was the last person she wanted to see at that moment let alone have a conversation with. She was hoping to avoid him this morning as her shift ended in a couple minutes.

"Missy? What's going on? Why'd you disappear?" asked Alan as he passed through the swinging produce doors.

"Disappear? What do you mean? My shift's over. You know Mr. Helovich hates overtime. I need to get this rack back downstairs and clock out." She could not even look him in the eye when she replied to him and nervously straightened up items on the rack.

"That's not what I meant. About us, two weeks ago? Why did you just disappear and ignore my texts and calls?"

Missy continued to avoid his gaze as she peeked in through the small window to see if the elevator had arrived yet. "It's nothing. Just forget that night! Please? I need to go."

"Forget it? How do I do that? We were having a great time and the next morning you vanished. No note. Nothing. I was stuck at Management Training for the last two weeks in Sacramento, wondering what I did wrong?" That was what bothered Alan the most: The fact that she did not even return his calls or texts. She ghosted him. Not even a "get lost" text. That would have been at least something to go on. He was starting to think maybe he was so drunk he just imagined it all.

"There was no connection. Ok! You want to know what happened? Fine, I'll tell you. You fell asleep on me. Makes a girl feel really special in the heat of passion to have the guy pass out on her."

The elevator door opened. She tugged on the cart as she started to back into the elevator. Alan lunged at her, grabbing at her arm hard and attempting to pull her back.

"What the... Get your hands off me!" demanded Missy as she attempted to break his grip.

"Missy! Stop!" Alan's frantic expression and desperate tone surprised Missy as she struggled to pull away from him. "Look behind you." This time his tone was calm and caring but he continued to keep a firm grip on her arm.

She looked behind and saw that the elevator doors had opened wide but the elevator itself was not there. It was just a large black hole into emptiness. She stopped struggling and jumped into his arms instead. "Oh, my god! Thank you. Luigi warned me the elevator was acting weird this morning but I didn't expect this."

He held her tight. The moment was perfect, and he had to go for it. "Give me another chance. Please? I promise I won't fall asleep on you. Come on. Just for dinner. Tonight? I'm buying. It's my lunch break so I'll have to eat and run anyways. We'll have some great food and just chat. Same place as two weeks ago? Around 8pm?"

Missy looked back into the empty pit and then back at Alan. His desperate plea for her to accept his invitation was pathetic, but she never passed up a free meal. "In this position, do I really have a choice? So, yes. I'll give you another chance. But Dinner Only. Nothing else."

"Dinner it is! Have to get up to see the boss right now, but I'll see you tonight for DINNER ONLY and nothing else. I understand." Alan turned and sprinted up the stairs to the manager's office.

Missy pushed the elevator button again, and this time, the elevator ascended from the basement even with the doors wide open. She pushed the cart onto the elevator, then reached in to push the down button. She never stepped into the elevator. Her arm barely missed being crushed as the elevator doors slammed shut. Missy walked around to the other side of the elevator where a doorway led down into the basement and she disappeared down the stairs.

Alan reached the top of the stairs and stood on a small landing where two doors stood. The one in front was the manager's office, while the one on the right was the door to the employee's break room, which was closed. That door should never be closed, crossed Alan's mind, so he decided to investigate. He slowly opened the door and peered in. He saw Peli asleep on top of one of the tables.

"Hey Peli, why are you up here? Didn't you just start your shift?"

"I'm on my break. Managers aren't allowed to harass us while we're on our breaks. Union rules, so leave me alone." She turned away from him and curled up into a fetal position.

"Union rules? I'll need to read up on that one. You just got here and were just bagging a big order for Paul. Did you even finish it?" asked Alan.

"I finished the price check he asked for and now it's my scheduled break."

"That's after you work two hours, you were late dropping Lily off at daycare, you said."

One of Peli's eyes opened, and she turned back to look at him. "Unless you have some emergency like a cleanup or we're out of baskets, I'm finishing my break." The one eye closed and she turned back to her sleeping position.

"Excuse me, but you dropped something."

Peli's eyes opened again. Her head tilted up off the table a little. "What did I drop?"

"Your footsteps!" Alan laughed.

Peli did not show any emotional response to the joke.

"That's your mother's joke for the day. Ms. Chili Pepper is hot today entertaining the customers."

She flipped him off with both of her middle fingers and then curled back up into a ball. "She's not my mother—just the vagina I fell out of, and that doesn't make her a mother."

Alan stared at her. What a useless bagger. He would have been fired for doing that when he was a bagger, but not her. Alan figured it might be because she was a single parent, and it would be difficult to fire her without tons of paperwork and probation hearings with the Union. She was good at avoiding work, but great at avoiding being written up, and that frustrated him. But actually, he felt sorry for her. The struggle she must experience every day to raise a child on a bagger's salary in this city must be overwhelming. He knew how hard it was surviving on that salary just by himself. To have another being to take care of, was more than Alan wanted to think about. He was not going to be the one to put her and Lily out on the street. He would just let her rest.

"Shh. Break, remember? I hear you breathing." Her voice was soft. She lay there motionless.

Alan turned from the doorway of the breakroom but did not close the door. He now faced the Manager's Office door. He stalled at the door for a moment to collect his thoughts. You always needed to mentally prepare yourself when dealing with Mr. Helovich. You never knew what to expect from him, a backhanded compliment or a direct insult.

He rapped on the door three times quickly, then paused, then knocked two more times. It was something that Mr. Helovich told all employees to do. If everything was okay, knock with that pattern. But, if there was something wrong, being held by gunpoint by a robber or something similar, Mr. Helovich instructed them to knock with four quick raps.

Mr. Helovich's voice blasted through the door. "It's about time!"

Alan opened the door and cautiously walked in.

The manager's office was designed like a nest, perched high in the store's corner so the boss could watch all of the activities below. Mr. Helovich had installed the one-way mirrors a couple of years ago, because he did not like customers and employees looking back at him. He wanted to watch them but did not like them watching him. There were some hooks along the wall to hang a couple of coats or hats. A large desk was covered with piles of paperwork scattered about. There were two chairs setup next to the desk. On the back wall was a large curtain which Alan knew was not there two weeks ago when he left for training.

Mr. Helovich was a mature, wild-eyed, hairy gray gorilla, with a huge head and belly and long, thick, hairy arms. He pulled Alan completely into his office and practically threw him in a chair.

Alan cowered at first as Mr. Helovich stood over him but sat up more confidently as he noticed his boss' dress shirt was half-tucked into his pants and chunks of food were stuck to his shirt and tie.

"Mr. Cherry, why are you late? Do you think now that you're an Assistant Manager you can just walk in here whenever you damn well feel like it, huh?" The entire time he spoke, Alan flinched as bits and pieces of food flew from Mr. Helovich's mouth and hit him or near him every time he spoke.

"I'm not scheduled until 1:00 pm, sir."

"What time is it now?"

Alan looked at the wall clock over the coat hooks. "Umm, 1:03, sir"

"Precisely. You are late. That is the time you are to be on the floor working. Where are you now? In my office talking to me. I expect you here prior to your start time, so I can give you your tasks for the day. You are to hit the floor at your scheduled time. You're not in the Union anymore, Boy! This is where the real men play, so suck it up, or take your toys with you and go back to being a lonely ass checker again."

"Yes, sir. I understand, and I will not do it again. I was late. Sorry." Alan said obediently.

Mr. Helovich looked Alan over closely like a gorilla would inspect another gorilla, wondering if it should attack or pick off bugs . Mr. Helovich even sniffed a couple of times while checking over Alan.

Satisfied, Mr. Helovich turned and walked over to the curtains on the back wall. "Let me show you something, my son." His tone was proud and anxious to share. He slid the curtains to one side and revealed a collection of security monitors which viewed the most common areas around the store: various locations on the main floor; the front, back, and side entrances; the loading dock; key locations in the basement; and even the parking lot. "What do you think?"

Alan stood up and approached the monitors to take a closer look. The clarity amazed him; as well as no one seemed to be aware of the cameras.

"I had them installed last week. They just finished connecting power to the monitors this morning. Now, I will know exactly who is ripping me off; customers or employees. I will now have the evidence to prosecute them."

One camera showed a customer in a motorized chair, wearing a large floppy sun hat, examining a carton of eggs. The lady dropped one of the eggs on the floor, looked around, and then dropped the entire carton to the floor. She then drove off in her chair.

Alan opened the Manager's door and yelled out, "Peli, clean up in front of the egg section."

From the break room, Peli yelled back, "Break, remember?"

"Now," Mr. Helovich yelled.

"On it, Mr. Helovich!" She flew out of the break room and down the stairs.

Alan was a little disturbed that she did not listen to him, but no one dared to ignore Mr. Helovich. Alan closed the door and return to examining the other new monitors.

"Sit down, Alan. About your schedule today. You will work with each department's manager today and observe what they do and how they do it. None of the corporate bullshit theories of how corporate thinks it should be done. Got it? You need to experience it for real and from those who are the experts in their areas. You will need to cover for them if they are sick or gone for lunch. Produce. Bakery. Meat. Dairy. Frozen Foods. And of course, the front booth operations."

"But..."

"No, Buts. It is actual work for you now, Mr. Cherry. No more fun and games. Now go as I need to find out what happened with the night crew. They never clocked out this morning and the dairy load was left on the loading dock instead of being moved into the dairy box. But the rest of the store appears to be completely stocked and faced up."

"Do you think they are druggies like the last night crew and just walked out?"

"No," replied Mr. Helovich sharply. "Mike was very confident they weren't into drugs and he doesn't show any signs of being a drug user himself. I have a nose for these things."

"Did it spoil? Would you like me to dump the load?"

"No need. I had Darci move it into the dairy box already. It should be cool again by now and ready for the shelves. You are leaving, correct, or should we continue with this tea party?"

Alan nodded at Mr. Helovich and closed the door behind him as he left. Alan thought he heard some grunting behind him as he left the office and imagined Mr. Helovich rushing up behind him pounding his chest like he was protecting his territory, just like those wildlife documentaries he watched about gorillas in high school science class.

CHAPTER 6

Fruits & Veggies Training

own below in the basement, past the cardboard baler and next to the Produce elevator, was the area designated for the Produce Department. Several rows of pallets held Russet potatoes, bananas, sweet potatoes, and various other non-refrigerated produce. A large, stainless-steel sink was where the vegetable trimming occurred: cleaning them up, soaking them in water, and then placing them in trays. Employees would then stack up the trays and slide them into the cold box. Throughout the day, produce clerks would pull out trays of various lettuces and bring them up to the main floor, placing them onto the wet racks for sale.

On the top shelf of the sink, a radio was playing classic rock-n-roll music. A dark, tanned, masculine, well-aged Italian man was trimming lettuce while he danced and sang along. Though he was a stocky man, it was not due to fat. His naturally muscular build was developed from years of working in the Produce Department, lifting and moving heavy boxes around. His gold chains and chest hair practically jumped into your face since he had unbuttoned the top two buttons of his work shirt as well as wore the rubber apron low around his neck. He was trimming heads of lettuce, wrapping them, and tossing them into the trays. He put a lot of hip thrusting and butt squeezing into his dance moves when alternating from slow to fast movements, all the while, juggling the head lettuce from the box, trimming it, tossing it into the water for a rise, and then popping a different one out to wrap it up and finally tossing it into a tray. A choreographed effort.

Alan walked around the corner and stopped for a moment while he watched Luigi dance. After a moment or two, he noticed Luigi's dance moves went from dancing to more like humping the sink itself.

"Are you going to just watch or join in with me?" asked Luigi without missing a beat.

"Luigi, you've got me on all the dance moves, that's for sure." Alan walked up and sat on a pallet which only had 3 layers of banana boxes on it.

"I do private lessons, if you like."

"What about your husband?"

"He can watch." Luigi continued dancing to the music but turned towards Alan as if he was performing for him.

"I'm here to learn all about the fruits and veggies."

"Isn't that what we're already talking about?" Luigi asked.

"Mr. Helovich said I have to learn from all of the department managers, so I thought I'd start with you."

"Alan! So, you chose me to be your very first. I am so honored. I will be gentle. I promise."

"Why is everything sexual with you?"

"I like to see if I can get you to blush. You're so innocent. It reminds me when I was your age and so naïve."

"I don't understand why he wants me to train in every department again. I've worked all of them for a couple of years now." Alan was frustrated that he had to go back to all these managers and be instructed again, even though he had already been trained; it was embarrassing.

"But you were just untrained by Corporate and he wants to trained by to the way he likes it. Don't worry, I've seen how you handle yourself with the fruits and how you care about the vegetables that roll in here. You're very respectful to everyone and everything. That's why everyone loves you."

Alan got up from the short stack of banana boxes and started removing their tops. He rolled back the thin plastic that covered the bananas inside the box. "Not everyone. Grace doesn't love me. She hates my guts. Oh, and now Missy, I think she hates me too. I'll break down the banana pallets for you."

"Dragon Lady and the Ice Queen. Wow! You know how to pick them, don't you? Maybe you should come over and play on my team for a while and avoid all that drama?" Luigi grabbed an empty pallet and carried it over to an empty spot next to Alan and tossed it onto the floor.

"I'll keep that in mind, but my team is fine."

"They're pretty green, so just unwrap one pallet and leave the other pallets covered so the bananas ripen faster." Luigi returned to the sink and started trimming some butter lettuce now.

Alan continued to unwrap the bananas in each box. He then carried the boxes over and placed them onto the empty pallet. "I'm pretty green myself. I need to figure out why I keep striking out with the girls."

"Well, Grace is ancient and very fragile, she's beyond a cougar. More like a Dragon Lady. You'll break her as soon as you touch her. Now for Missy, I didn't know you two were involved."

"We hooked up the night before I left for training. If you can call it a hook up. We ran into each other in the bar at Vinnie's restaurant, on the corner of Powell and California. The next thing I know, we're in my apartment. I'm stripped down and sitting on my bed and I can remember her standing there in my bathroom." Alan paused for a moment as he struggled to remove the top from one last banana box.

"Then? You can't stop there. You're teasing me with that image in my head. Then what happened?"

Alan looked disappointed as he knew what was next and was embarrassed by it. "I don't know. I woke up the next morning. She was gone. I blacked out. I tried calling her, but she never answered and never called me back. I didn't think I was that drunk. I slept through my alarm and was going to miss my train to Sacramento for training, so I couldn't stop by her place. We haven't spoken 'til this morning at work. She said I fell asleep on her, so she left."

"Asleep, huh? Well, my team wouldn't have left you all alone. You would have woken up either tied up or chained up and very sore. Depends," responded Luigi as he looked off in the distance and imagined Alan tied up and in chains.

"Can you at least keep my clothes on when I'm in your imagination? It's a little chilly right now." Alan was finally able to loosen the top of the banana box. He pulled back the plastic, then jumped back as he realized there was a large, black, furry tarantula sitting on the top of the bananas.

The spider jumped onto his chest and he screamed like a little girl while dancing around in a circle as he tried to shake it off.

Luigi started laughing at Alan as he watched him dance around. He grabbed a small whisk broom and walked over to Alan. Luigi started dancing in sync with Alan while he raised the broom into the air. "You scream like a little girl. Stop moving."

Alan froze for a moment as a little whine resonated from his nose, and then Luigi swung the broom at Alan's chest. The spider shot off his chest and onto the floor. It turned around and stared back at them; then disappeared immediately under the pallet.

"Did you see the size of that thing? It tried to eat me!" whined Alan.

"They're harmless. Get a grip. I told you spiders hide in those boxes. You didn't believe me, did you?"

"It's so big and ugly. Where'd it go? We've got to kill it."

"Do you always kill big ugly things the first time you meet them? Heck, I would have killed my last three partners if I did that. It'll die soon. Bananas are gassed before they're shipped just for this reason. You're safe now. Just calm down."

"I'm done here. Thanks. I'm going top side. I need a donut or something. I'll come back when you show me the dead carcass of that furry villain." Alan cautiously walked down the aisleway, scanning the bottoms of the pallets and any cracks or spaces in the pallets where spiders might hide. He actually moved some of the dollies and pushed them into a pallet to see if anything moved. When he reached the stairs, he sprinted up them.

CHAPTER 7

Tasty Creations

In the very back corner of the basement wall, Mike shuffled out of the hole. His movements were extremely stiff and uncoordinated. He turned and walked into the wall. The Lemures struggled to control his movements and work in unison as each limb was controlled by a different creature. His eyes were swollen and red and his overall appearance was scruffy and covered in dirt.

He grabbed some empty potato sacks off the shelf next to the boxes of film and attempted to recover the hole, so it wouldn't be noticed. He stumbled along the way. Let me control my body and we'd get there faster, he thought in his head, hoping the Lemures would hear him. But how could they since all they were doing was giggling every time he ran into the wall or fell on his face.

He opened the chain-link gate and then closed it behind him but set the lock back in place without locking it. Anyone inspecting the lock would see it was unlocked, but from a distance, it would appear to be locked.

He walked over to one of the motorized pallet movers and placed his hand over the engine. A couple of Lemures slid out from his sleeves and dropped onto it. They melted into the electric motor and it started up and began to move slowly on its own. A couple more Lemures dropped out the bottom of Mike's pants and ran head on into the pallet mover and were absorbed into it. The device began to move faster than usual.

◆ ◆ ◆

Mr. Helovich was reviewing the inventory, orders, and sales reports for the week. The reports showed that the order quantities were up compared to last year, but when he crossed reference them with sales and remaining inventory, there was a major shortage. Inventory was disappearing. It appeared that over a hundred thousand dollars was missing. He was well aware that the previous night crew was stealing from him. He had fired them and hired Mike and his buddies who he thought to be honest, ex-military guys that just needed a break. Mr. Helovich rarely went with the soft heart approach, but there was something about Mike that prompted him to say yes. He did not remember what that reason was but he knew it must have been a good one. It was strange though, he thought, that he could not remember the details since he had always remembered why he hired or fired someone. Even with the change of the night crew, he was still losing money and the inventory numbers indicated that it was disappearing in large quantities.

Mr. Helovich looked up at the monitors in frustration from what the reports were showing him. He noticed Mike on one of the monitors in the basement. He could see stacks of liquor and cigarettes in the cage in the background. Mr. Helovich was furious as his first thought, from Mike's scruffy appearance, was that he had passed out all night from drinking the booze in the locked cage. "You bastard, you are a druggy! You're fired!" Mr. Helovich blurted out at Mike on the monitor as he smashed his fist down onto his desk, sending all the reports flying into the air. "Where's the record button, where is it?" He searched frantically for it.

Mike seemed to mentally hear Mr. Helovich's outburst as he turned and looked directly into the camera. His face grew large as he moved closer to the lens. Then the signal went dead and only static came over the monitor.

"Damn him!" screamed Mr. Helovich. "Stealing and damaging company property. Mister, you are done here." He darted over to the Manager's door and locked it. Then he went to the coat rack and pulled the third hook down. A secret door opened and revealed stairs leading below.

◆ ◆ ◆

Alan walked into the Bakery and straightened up the tables as he scanned for something to eat. He stopped and looked at Baker Bob. It was a replica of a short, portly baker holding a sign of the daily specials. His eyes were life-like and seemed to follow you around the room.

"Hello, Baker Bob. How's business today?" asked Alan. He noticed a little girl in the shopping cart staring at him while her mother was discussing a cake order with the Bakery clerk. "What was that Baker Bob?" Alan glanced over to see that the little girl was watching him closely as he talked to the little statue. "Oh, you've made too many donuts and they will spoil. Really? Hum, we can't have that." Alan opened the donut case and pulled out two chocolate old fashioned donuts and took a bite out of one of them, and then looked over at the little girl whose eyes were fixed on the donut in his other hand. He handed that donut to the little girl. Her eyes widened with excitement as she had to use both hands to hold it tight. He took the other donut out of his mouth and put his index finger to his lips so the little girl would be quiet. She nodded her head in agreement and then started devouring the donut.

Alan walked around the counter to the back side and passed behind the Bakery clerk who was finishing up the cake order for the mother of the little girl. He heard the mother's squeal as she saw chocolate smeared all over her daughter's face. "How did you get that!" she demanded. The little girl looked around, but Alan was gone, so she pointed to Baker Bob. "I don't think so. No candy at the register for you, young lady," declared the mother, as she pulled out a baby wipe from her purse and started rubbing the chocolate streaks off the little girl's face and hands.

When he reached the back of the bakery, Alan realized Bill was expecting him and he was dressed in his full baker's outfit, an all-white apron, hat, and pants. His roundness was typical of a baker as they are supposed to taste all of their creations. Bill had laid out various types of frozen pastries on several cooking trays, which were spread out over the wooden baking table.

Alan finished his last bite of the chocolate donut and sat down at the table.

"Mr. Cherry, already starting your training, I see. Awesome! Lesson one, always taste your creations. It's the only way to know if it's good enough for consumer consumption, but you can't sit down now," said Bill. "You're baking. Place those trays on the baking rack."

"Come on, Bill, it's just Alan. Is Mr. Helovich making all you guys do this to me? I don't think you'd like being called Mr. Bill, Mr. Bill. Mr. Bill? Oh, Forget it. Old reruns." Alan stood up and grabbed a tray and slipped it into the baking rack. Then another tray and another. All trays were loaded up into the rack in only a couple of minutes, so Alan sat back down.

"Good job."

"So, what fun stuff do we get to mix up in that big blender behind you? I've only been able to help on the counter, never back here to make anything" asked Alan as he was looking around at all the various appliances.

"That thing?" asked Bill, as he walked over to it and laid his hands on it, as if it was some sacred tool for a baker. "This is only for show. I haven't used it in a long time. We just have it there, so customers think we are actually making everything from scratch on site."

"But Baker Bob's sign says it is all from scratch."

"Yes, that's true, everything is made from scratch somewhere, just not here at the store." Bill threw a box onto the table. "Here you go. Make more pastries. Take the frozen pucks out of the box and creatively lay them out on the cooking trays. Then, grab another cooking rack and load them up and we'll roll them into the oven. I'll roll the first rack in now as it is already loaded. Voila! Fresh pastries."

Alan started arranging the frozen pastries on the cooking sheets. No matter how he turned them or laid them out, they all looked the same.

Bill rolled the rack over to the walk-in oven and opened the door.

"This isn't incredibly fun. A monkey could do this," complained Alan.

Bill positioned the rack in the center of the oven, locked it in place, and then closed the door.

"Excuse me? What did you say?"

Bill turned the oven on by turning a dial and then hitting a large green button. The rack started to turn, and it sounded like a fan turned on inside the oven itself.

"Nothing. Doesn't this get boring?" Alan was hoping to see something new in this area since his previous training was to just to grab the trays in the backroom and push them up front to the counter. He wanted to do some real baking, which would be more exciting than arranging frozen pucks and pushing them into a rotating oven. Then patiently sitting and waiting for the bell to go off just so you can finally pull them out and roll *them* up to the front counter. Boring.

"Sure, but what can I do? All the stores do it this way now. No money to open my own bakery and compete against them, so I settled for the appearance of being a baker. I get benefits, at least with the Union."

Alan noticed another machine with many blades next to the other wall. "What about that machine over there?" He pointed to a device behind Bill. "It has crumbs on it, so that one is still used. Or are those fake crumbs to look like we used it?"

"Oh, that. It's a bread slicer. In case the customers want their French bread sliced. No reason you need training on that. A monkey could do it."

♦ ♦ ♦

Mike released several more Lemures in the basement. The more Lemures that left his body, the more control he gained back. They rapidly disappeared in different directions.

The spider from the banana box dropped from the ceiling and onto Mike's shoulder. He calmly reached up and picked it off him, then placed it on the ground. Just before releasing it, Mike started convulsing and opened his mouth. A portly Lemure squeezed out and landed directly on the spider. The spider wildly tried to escape, but the gooey Lemure wrapped itself around the spider and slowly absorbed into it. The spider stopped moving for a moment, appeared to be dead, then stood up. It disappeared underneath a pallet.

CHAPTER 8

Darci's Milk

A lan was walking down the frozen food aisle when a customer approached him from behind to ask him a question.

"Excuse me, sir?" asked a guy who was not much older than Alan himself, dressed in dirty sweats, an oversized t-shirt and flip-flops.

Alan stopped and cheerfully turned to assist him. He noticed the growing aroma of something rotting or decaying in the air. He wondered if it was coming from the customer himself, or perhaps another customer had released it and left the area. "What can I help you with?" He slowed his breathing to reduce the intake of any fouler air.

"Can you tell me where the BBQ sauce is?"

"Sure, it's two aisles over that way. What brand or type?" asked Alan who continued to see if the customer showed any signs of smelling the toxic gas that was emanating from the area. Alan's eyes were about to start watering if he stayed there any longer.

"Honey Jalapeño," he said, as he pulled a piece of paper from his hand basket and read his list.

"That's in the organic section. That's three aisles over in the other direction, one third down on your left side. It should be on the third shelf from the top.

"Wow, that's pretty impressive. What about lighter fluid?"

"For barbecuing or cigarettes?"

"Oh, you're good. Cigarettes." He responded as he fought back a grin

as he attempted to keep Alan there as long as possible.

"Aisle four, at the front of the store on the right side, very top shelf. Photographic memory."

"Wow, impressive. Thanks," responded the guy.

As Alan walked away, he noticed the customer's basket already had both the BBQ sauce and lighter fluid, despite the questions he had just answered. was asking about their locations.

Why do customers do that? thought Alan. Why do they torture me so much?

He looked back at the customer only to realize the customer was staring at his ass.

Embarrassed by being caught for staring, the customer retreated towards the other end of the aisle while he repeatedly flatulated as he scurried off.

The regular noise of the store with customers talking and the over-head page announcements continued, but none of them called for Alan directly, so he ignored them.

Along the back wall, just past the Meat Department, was the dairy section. The refrigeration system was much older and completely an open design; no doors enclosed the products. Rows of yogurt, sour cream, coffee creamers, and eventually milk continued to the end of the back wall.

An impressive business executive, dressed in a tailored gray suit, moved a couple of milk cartons to the side and looked in towards the back of the dairy case.

"Hey Darci. Do you get a break soon? We could chat in my car if you like. Like last time?" He asked while using his suave and confident tone.

"I told you. I'm not interested. You're married. You lied to me," responded a tantalizing female voice from the back side of the dairy case. Even though the voice was saying no, the tone did not quite reflect the words.

"Come on, you said you enjoyed it very much. You blew my mind. No one has ever done that to me before. It was incredible."

"Go home to your wife! Let her blow your brains out," responded the bodiless voice. Still, the tone was more teasing than upset.

"Darci! Please come out here and talk to me," demanded the executive.

Alan walked up and stood directly next to the man and stared at him. "Is there a problem, Sir?"

He looked Alan up and down and assessed him for a moment. He puffed up his chest at Alan as he read Alan's name tag and the Assistant Manager title on it.

"Not finding everything on your wife's list, Mr. Harper? I can help Mrs. Harper on Saturday morning when she does her regular shopping if you can't find something."

That seemed to deflate his growing territorial threat towards Alan as he released his breath and his chest deflated back to normal.

"You've got bitter-sour milk back there," complained Mr. Harper as he walked off clipping Alan's shoulder and then left the store.

Alan could barely see the exit at the front of the store but he stared after Mr. Harper the entire time to confirm that he left. Once he was convinced that Mr. Harper was not returning, he turned to the dairy case and investigated the hole the guy had been speaking into.

"You really need to be more selective on your choices or you'll end up on the back of one of these milk cartons one day." He pointed to the picture of a missing woman on the back of a carton.

"Shut up and get your ass in here, Mr. Cherry. It is training time for you, little boy." The voice became enticing and commanding while retaining its earlier sensual tone.

"Yes, ma'am."

Several pallets of milk crates and dairy products lined the back wall of the refrigerator including various types of milk, yogurts, sour creams, and cottage cheeses.

Darci was unloading the dairy load from the night before, the delivery that Mike had left out on the loading dock overnight. Her blonde hair bounced around as she danced provocatively to the music in her headset. She had the typical olive-colored grocery apron that everyone else wore in the store, but like Missy's, it did not quite match everyone else's. In Darci's case, it was her watermelon-size breasts which caused the apron to pull up and appear short as her western jeans snugged her curvy hips like an upside-down heart-shaped ass.

The door to the refrigerated Dairy Box opened. Alan walked in and instantly felt the wall of cool air. Darci was filling from the backside of the dairy case with product by pushing the items to the front of the shelves. Her back was to Alan. He closed the door slowly and stood there for a moment, watching as she enjoyed listening to her music on her headset. He attempted to guess what song was playing based on her dance moves. Both she and Luigi could definitely move their bodies with the music.

"So, who do you enjoy watching dance more, me or Luigi?" asked Darci as if she could read his mind. She pulled the plugs out of her ears and continued stocking the back of the dairy case, continuing to dance to the music in her mind.

"What? What are you talking about?"

"Since you won't ask me out on a date, I just figured you liked Luigi better than me. It's okay. Really, I understand. What other reason could there be? I've got everything a guy wants and yet you don't want any of it." She turned and faced Alan as she delivered her last statement and moved in a way to emphasize her breasts, tilting her head as she raised one of her eyebrows.

Alan was not sure how to respond to that challenge, since he thought she was beautiful, with her long, curly, honey-blonde hair and curvy body. But, her interest in men changed daily with whomever caught her eye. Alan knew that if they went out together anywhere, he would have to deal with all the other guys she had dated before or slept with. "That's not true. Darci, how about we focus on dairy training only? We can address the other stuff another time, okay? Please."

Darci looked him up and down as she walked around him and assessed him, and she would 'hum' and 'ha' as she focused on certain parts of his body. "So serious. You're just like Mr. Helovich. All work. No fun. No play. Fine. Break down the milk load. I'm finishing up on the variety products and need to get most of it on the shelves."

Alan exhaled as her inspection of his body concluded. He walked back to the dairy door and grabbed a large metal hook which was hanging on the back of it, then walked over to the first pallet of milk and attached the hook to the bottom of a stack of milk crates and slid it off the pallet. He dragged the stack to the back wall and lined them up a step or so out from the wall. He continued creating rows of milk crates, blue tops in one row, red tops in another. This continued until Alan had all the crates off the pallets and separated into rows by same colored tops. "What am I learning here? I do this every time I work the diary load. Nothing new here."

"Yes, but this time it is 'official' training. The boss can actually write you up now since he has proof we have trained you in each department. That's all the documentation he needs so he can fire you if you don't do it the correct way. See it as an insurance policy for him for when he wants to fire you and you don't follow one rule. Before, the Union protected you, and it didn't matter if your training was documented or not. Now, he can fire you on the spot and accuse you of not doing it by the "company policies" which by the way, we don't train you that way." She slid a small stack of milk crates to the left side of Alan's stacks, then turned her head back to look at him while bending over the stack. "Personally, a young stud like yourself with all your muscles should want to help me make a milkshake." She winked at him.

♦ ♦ ♦

Luigi pulled a pallet of iceberg lettuce out of the produce cold box and parked it just in front of the trimming table. He kept the motorized pallet mover engaged in the pallet and walked around to the other side. He lifted off the top box and threw it onto the trimming table. He then reached for the knife in his side belt holder and noticed it was missing. Luigi looked on the table and on the surrounding floor. He did not see his trimming knife anywhere. He entered the cold box and scanned the area to see where he might have dropped it.

Mike entered the area while Luigi was in the cold box. He walked up to the lettuce pallet still parked next to the trimming table. A couple of Lemures slid down his arm and onto the motorized pallet mover. They melted into the mechanical device.

A hidden door opened behind the large cardboard baler across from the produce area and Mr. Helovich slipped out. He paused for a moment as he peered around the baler and spotted Mike. He remained motionless as he watched Mike.

Luigi walked out of the produce box, holding his trimming knife, and slipped it back into his belt holder. He didn't notice Mike standing off to the side.

Luigi walked over to the pallet and picked up a box of iceberg lettuce and placed it on the table to trim. He ripped off the top and pulled out a couple of heads of lettuce. He began trimming, then tossed them into the sink. One head bounced and dropped onto the ground, so Luigi turned and kneeled to pick it up just as the lettuce rolled away. While he reached for it, a large black work boot stepped down and stopped it.

Luigi gazed up and was met with Mike's grinning face. "Hey, Mike." He stood up gradually and returned the grin. A long moment of silence passed as the two men stared back at each other.

Mike's left eyebrow unintentionally rose for a moment. Then, his head nodded towards the produce box, again not of his own will. He winked at Luigi. Now, Mike knew the Lemures were fucking with him and Luigi. He could do nothing to stop it, though. He struggled to take control of his body again, but to no avail.

Luigi's grin changed to an enormous smile. He tossed the lettuce over his shoulder without even looking behind him, and it landed in the sink. He walked over to the cold box and turned back to Mike. "So, you're the quiet grunting type, solider man? Just step inside, stand at attention, and I'll do the rest." He pushed open one of the swinging doors and slipped in.

Through the plastic windows on the swinging rubber doors, Luigi descended onto his knees to wait in anticipation for Mike's entrance. He noticed Mike wink back at him as he descended into position.

Mike stepped to the side as the pallet mover, with the stack of head lettuce boxes on it, shot directly into the cold box. As the doors swung open, Mike could see Luigi on his knees directly in line of the speeding pallet mover. It plowed directly into him. Luigi's muffled screams did not last long as the pallet pinned him underneath and dragged his body to the back wall crushing him. Blood oozed out from under the swinging doors.

Mike then calmly walked, still not under his own control, into the produce box.

Mr. Helovich watched the entire event from behind the cardboard baler. The shock caused him to inhale so quickly that he thought his gasp gave him away, but Mike entered the box at just the same time. Mr. Helovich carefully tiptoed backwards a few steps to the hidden door but then tripped and landed on his knees and hands.

The hiding spider jumped onto the back of his hand and bit him. He screamed and instinctively smashed it with his other hand. He wiped off the gooey guts and noticed the back of his hand had a large, bloody bite mark.

The cold box door swung wide open and Mike stepped out, looking around.

Mr. Helovich held his breath and tried not to move but the pain from spider bite was intense. Once satisfied that no one was in the area, Mike returned back inside the cold box.

Mr. Helovich lifted his massive gorilla body off the floor and headed to the hidden door, slipped in, and quietly latched it shut.

◆ ◆ ◆

Grace was counting money from several stacked cash drawers in the Front Booth. She began to feel oddly faint, then staggered and fell, knocking a cash drawer onto the floor. She pulled herself up and moved over to a stool as she attempted to steady herself and sit down. The room seemed to sway back and forth as if she was on a boat at sea. She reached for the phone and dialed. It rang and rang. Nothing. She then pushed a button and spoke into the phone. "Mr. Helovich, Service 1, Service 1 at the Front Booth." Her announcement echoed as it repeated over the paging system.

Up in the manager's office, Mr. Helovich stumbled into the office from the secret door. He plopped his enormous body into the office chair. The force slid him and the chair up against the wall making a loud thud.

Another announcement went out over the paging system from Grace: '*Mr. Helovich, please call the Booth as soon as possible.*'

He picked up the phone and dialed 13, which was the extension for the Front Booth. "Grace, what is it? I'm busy right now. It better be important!"

Grace's voice was frail. "I'm not feeling well. I need to go home right now. You usually leave about this time. Could you take me to my apartment? It's on your way. I'm not sure I can make it alone."

Mr. Helovich could not remember one day in all the years that Grace worked at the store that she was ever sick. He wanted to help her home, but he looked at the spider bite on the back of his hand

and it was already showing some green pus along the edges. "All of us get sick at work, but we stick it out 'til the end of our shift. I understand you're old. I get it. Are the books done for the week? No? Well, I expect you in early tomorrow morning to finish them then. Call Alan. Have him escort you home. I have something I need to take care of so I'm not leaving for a while yet." He hung up on her without waiting for her response. Mr. Helovich watched as the gooey infection spread up his arm. His head sweated profusely.

'*Alan, please call the booth. Alan, please,*' echoed over the paging system. That was the last thing Mr. Helovich said as he turned to a small mirror on the wall and watched the poison traveling up his neck, and then the room spun, and he blacked out.

◆ ◆ ◆

Alan was stacking up empty pallets in the corner of the Dairy Box since he had completed breaking down the rest of the dairy load. Several announcements came across the paging system. It was not clear what they were about since the noise from stacking the pallets blocked it out.

He threw up the last pallet to the top of the stack when another announcement came in over the paging system. Grace's voice clearly stated, '*Alan, please call the Booth. Mr. Cherry, please report to the Front Booth. Service 1.'*

"Looks like your next lesson is about to begin. Better get your cute little ass up there before she croaks on you. Don't forget, I'm here for you anytime you want some more personal training on those muscles of yours." Darci put her headset back on and continued stocking the back of the dairy case.

Alan expressed relief, "Finally, something I haven't done before." He darted out of the Dairy Box.

CHAPTER 9

Saving the Dutch

Alan sprinted out of the dairy box and pushed open the two swinging doors which led out to the main floor. Unbeknownst to him, he almost pushed the swinging doors into the female customer who was usually found reading the magazines along the checkstands. She was approaching the doors when they flung open unexpectantly. Alan continued up to the front lobby, unaware of the close collision. The female customer stopped the door in time to keep it from hitting her in the face. She watched as the young clerk did not even stop or noticed her. That's fine, I'll just complain to the manager later, she thought to herself. She had to use the restroom at the moment and was focused on that.

She passed through the swinging doors and into the back room. "Excuse me? Anyone back here? I am looking for the bathroom. Hello?" she asked as she slowly walked through the backroom, looking for the restrooms. She approached the produce freight elevator as there seemed to be a slight banging noise coming from inside it. As she approached it, the elevator doors slowly opened.

"Hello, I'm looking for the bathroom," she said again. As the doors completely opened, she noticed the empty pit, where the elevator car should have been so she attempted to step back but bumped into something and turned around quickly.

Mike was standing directly behind her and she now faced him. His eyes were swollen red and his body was profusely perspiring., and A strange odor floated towards her and the smell hit her like a brick wall of rotting flesh. "Restroom?" said Mike as he stood inches from her.

She nodded.

"Let me show you," offered Mike as he turned away from her. But then turned back around with a crazed, evil grin. He grabbed her by the shoulders and shoved her backwards into the elevator shaft. She screamed and disappeared into the darkness. "Restrooms are for paying customers only. Sorry."

Two Lemures dropped out from the bottom of his pants and jumped into the black pit after her.

Deep within Mike's head, a voice screamed with rage and it grew louder and louder until he was able to distinguish it as Samael's voice. *This is taking forever,* Samael screamed in frustration, *Michael, release all of the Lemures now. I sense there's a virgin nearby. We need to complete this before the Dragon Spirit regains its strength. I'm sure you'd like the relief as well. Now hurry!* The voice faded but the pain it caused in his head lingered on.

Mike dropped to his knees and then to all fours, like a dog. His body shook and convulsed as most of the Lemures exited his body from all orifices. His screams were little whimpers as he fought to catch his breath from the gagging as each Lemure popped out of his mouth. Mike's evil features softened and returned him closer to his normal serious appearance. Although he still was disheveled looking as a result of a difficult night he had struggling with the Lemures inside him to control his body and lead them to the store. The Lemures scattered in all directions throughout the backroom and out onto the main shopping floor.

Over in the Meat Department, a customer in a motorized chair, with a full basket of groceries, flagged Alan down as he approached from the other end. "Excuse me, sir. Can you help me?"

Alan was sprinting up towards the front of the store to the Booth but could not avoid this customer as she moved her chair into the middle of the aisle. "Yes. Sure. What's up?" Alan asked, while he thought about Grace's page asking for him. She used "Mr. Cherry", a formal address which she has never used. What was happening at the Booth? Service 1 was an emergency. Why didn't she call for Mr. Helovich?

The customer drove a customized wheelchair which had been modified with a small shopping cart added to the front. She wore a flowery sundress, a large floppy straw hat, and red sunglasses that matched her high heel pumps. She dwarfed the wheelchair as she was well over six feet tall. Her creamy light chocolate skin revealed a perfect complexion that any woman would die for. Besides all of that, the only thing that seemed unusual about her was her prominent Adam's apple, thick knuckles, and size 13 pumps. "I want to check out your meat and measure the difference."

"I beg your pardon?" Alan said as that request had caught him off guard.

"Can you come closer? I can't reach it." She then pointed to a sign hanging on the meat rack. It read, 'Measure the THICKNESS yourself. You WON'T be disappointed.'

"Oh, here you go." Alan reached for the string hanging off the sign and pulled up a plastic ruler and handed it to her. She used the ruler on two pieces of steak in her basket.

"Thank you. Is your meat always freshly wrapped when you use it?" she said to him as she batted her extra-long, mascaraed eyelashes, while smiling. She then slowly raised the plastic ruler up and showed him a rather large condom which was covering the ruler. "Because this one looks like it's been used before."

"Oh my god. That's disgusting. Hey, you were that lady who dropped eggs on the floor this earlier today! I remember your hat and those large knuckles."

She threw a steak at Alan and then zipped by him on her motorized chair knocking him over into the meat counter.

"Hey!" Alan yelled as he fell into the counter.

The overhead page made its announcement again, but this time Grace's voice was extremely weak: '*Mr. Cherry, Service...*' The page cut out and stopped.

Alan picked up the package of meat that was now on the ground and tossed it back onto the meat counter. He then rushed to the front of the store.

♦ ♦ ♦

Darci continued arranging the dairy products into the back of the dairy shelves as she pushed the yogurt forward, filling it from behind. The door to the dairy box opened. Darci knew it had been opened and that someone had just entered because she felt the change in the air pressure. She had worked in this box for many years so she knew whenever someone entered, even though she had music playing on her headset. She would continue doing what she was doing and not show any signs that she was aware that she was not alone. Darci did not understand why the male psyche loved to scare women, so she always played along with the game and acted startled since it usually ended with a hug to calm her down. This gave her a chance to feel the guy's body and see how strong his arms were.

Darci went into her act as she turned around and jumped back, startled to see someone standing there at the door. Because of the positioning of the light in the dairy box, she could only view the outlined form of a person standing by the door. It wasn't until they stepped further into the box that she could see the detail of their features. In this case, she knew immediately who it was from the V-shape body and broad shoulders. It could only be one person. Darci had memorized that form and dreamt many times of seeing more of what was under his apron.

She approached him slowly, smiling as she thought this was the moment she had been waiting for. "Hello, Mike. So, the soldier returns to finish his mission. Did you bring your gun loaded? Let's just pick it up where we left off and don't be so shy this time. Just pull it out for me now."

She stepped between two tall stacks of milk crates and kneeled, so she would not be seen if someone walked into the dairy box.

"Come here, soldier. I'll oil up your gun and clean it fully while slowly torturing you to the very end."

Mike swaggered towards her. He stopped just in front of where she was kneeling. Her face was inches away from his crotch. He said nothing. From the lighting in the dairy box, she could not see much of his face.

"Oh, torturing me with the silent treatment now. But I know what you want." She reached up and lowered his zipper.

His hands reached down in front of her as if he was going to pull out his gun for her, but she pushed his hands to the side. "No, you don't! My mouth will do the searching and lock in on it." She noticed his pants grew outward, which showed her he was getting excited. She would take it nice and slow, she thought, since she wanted to drain every drop out of him.

Mike's hands moved to caressing her head which was covered with soft curly blonde hair. She loved his hands in her hair and she felt little pinpricks rush down her back. She leaned towards Mike and opened her mouth, sticking her tongue out as she anticipated finally witnessing Mike's manliness at any second.

A Lemure popped its head out from Mike's unzipped pants and revealed needle-like teeth. Darci's expression went from surprise to horror. She screamed as she attempted to scurry backward.

Mike's hands locked on Darci's head and he forced it deep into his crotch. She struggled at first. Her arms flailed. Some gooey Lemure dripped out of her nose and ears but then retreated back into her body. She went limp and stopped struggling. Mike took a step back from her while still clasping her head. He snapped her neck and her body slumped to the ground.

"Now, I'm totally relieved!" grunted Mike in an unnatural voice.

◆ ◆ ◆

The customer in the wheelchair turned down the cereal aisle and was busy looking back to see if Alan was pursuing her as she unknowingly ran over a Lemure. She stopped the chair right on top of the Lemure while looking up and down the aisle to make sure no one else was around. The Lemure absorbed into the chair while she paused to check one more time that the aisle was clear. She then took the remaining package of steaks and slipped it under her seat.

As she opened her seat, a can of beer fell out onto the floor and rolled underneath it, traveling some distance away as she shoved the steaks into the hidden compartment. She then sprung up from her seat and jogged to the beer to pick it up. As she bent over to snag up the beer, the motorized chair quickly ran into her and knocked her into the basket. The seat belts wrapped around her to keep her from getting out of the basket. The wheelchair then turned around and shot straight down the aisleway and blasted through the swinging doors to the backroom. She continued to struggle to get free, but the belts tightened around her arms. The chair approached the produce elevator which opened its doors. The chair, along with the customer in her flowery sundress, drove into the black void. Her floppy sunhat flew up into the air as they disappeared down into the pitch-black pit. The elevator shaft moaned as the hat landed partially on the edge of the floor. The sunhat balanced for a moment but finally tilted into the shaft following its owner.

♦ ♦ ♦

Alan knocked on the Front Booth's door. "Grace, are you in there? Grace?" he asked as he pounded on the door a couple more times. He pulled out a large key chain filled with various keys. He tried to unlock the door, but the key that should have unlocked the door did not work. He tried several other keys, but none of them worked.

"Grace, are you okay?" Still there was no answer. He wondered if she had finally croaked and was dead on the floor. He tried to force the doorknob while he threw his body into the door. His body bounced off it with no effect. "Shit, Mr. Helovich's going to kill me," as he rushed the door again and kicked it until it finally burst open.

Grace was sprawled out on the floor, motionless.

Alan rushed to her side and gently shook her. He listened for a heartbeat, but there was too much noise from the registers outside to hear anything else. He shook her harder. He then supported her head and neck as he bent over her to give her mouth-to-mouth resuscitation.

"Get away from me pervert!" responded Grace faintly. She attempted to push him away, but it was a struggle as she was weak. "Do you think I'm one of your hussies just waiting to get a kiss from you?" Once she pushed him back far enough from her, she attempted to stand up using the stool to pull herself up. She held onto the stool to stabilize herself and finally was firmly on her feet again.

"I thought you were dying or worse, dead." Alan's tone was caring and emotional, and she noticed his concern was honest and real.

She shyly looked away and mumbled, "Wish I could," then returned to the moment and looked back at him and grabbed his shoulder to keep from falling as she was still lightheaded. "I'm so embarrassed. I'm sorry. I don't know what happened. I need to go home. Can you take me? Please?"

Alan noticed for the first time that Grace had a tattoo of a green dragon on her shoulder and it appeared to wrap itself around the back of her neck. It also surprised him to see how smooth her skin was near the tattoo. The rest of her body was old, wrinkled and covered with age spots, but not around the tattoo. In fact, the colors of the tattoo were so vivid, he thought it almost looked as if it was a brand-new tattoo; definitely not a tattoo from her younger years, as it would have been all distorted and faded by now.

Grace noticed Alan staring at her neck and shoulder. She looked down and saw her shirt had shifted to the side, exposing her green dragon. She adjusted her shirt quickly and covered it back up.

"We should call an ambulance, or I'll drive you to the ER. You really should get checked out."

"NO!" snapped Grace. "I am okay. I just need to go home and rest. I'll come back tomorrow in the morning and finish the books."

Alan looked at the clock hanging in the Booth. It showed that it was thirteen minutes to seven p.m. He had time to drop her off and still get to the restaurant to meet Missy by eight o'clock. He turned back to Grace and smiled. "Yeah, I can take you home." He thought all of Grace's hair was white or gray, but he noticed she still had some very distinct streaks of black hair mixed in. Strange, he thought. He had never noticed that before. "But I'll only take you if you promise me you'll call 911 if you aren't feeling well again. Promise?"

"I promise," she said innocently and softly. "I didn't know you cared so much."

"Mr. Helovich will kill me if you don't come back to finish those books. Which I believe you were supposed to train me on them tonight. You can't die until you have a backup or he will kill you again in your grave. Hey, let me call him so he knows I'm taking you home and then going on my dinner break."

"No need to. He's the one who told me to call you."

"Well, let's get out of here before we get a rush of customers and he calls us back to help."

Alan assisted Grace as they walked out of the Booth and through the lobby to the front entrance. Grace leaned heavily onto Alan for support. It was the first time Alan was this close to her and he could smell the faint fragrance of lavender.

"I like what you've done with your hair. You look younger."

"What? I have done nothing to it. Are you really trying to sweet talk this old lady when I'm at my weakest? Not sportsman-like at all."

"No. That's not what I meant. Just relax and save your strength. Let's just get you home."

The entire front lobby was empty of customers and Paul stood in his checkout stand reading a gossip magazine.

"Paul, really? Don't just stand around. Face-up the front ends. Look busy while you're waiting for customers."

"Sorry, buddy. It was so busy just a second ago, but it suddenly just died off, so Mandy left for her break. No clue where Peli went."

"I need you to stay a little longer tonight if you can. I'm taking Grace home. She's not feeling well. Then I'm going on my dinner break. I'll be back around 9pm to close up and lock the doors. Then, you and Mandy can clock out. I'll stay to restock the displays and see if night crew shows up on time."

"No problem, boss. Oh, no playmates coming over tonight, so no moaning to listen to when you get home." He winked at Alan and started straightening up the candy along the checkstand.

Alan and Grace walked out of the store and into the damp, misty San Francisco evening which customarily embraced the parking lot. He directed her towards his car that was parked under the Food Mart sign. "My car is over here."

"No need to drive. I live across the street." She pointed to the apartment building. It was old and dilapidated.

Alan's heart saddened for a moment as it surprised him that she lived in a place like that. All the years she had worked for this store, he thought, she should have been able to afford a nicer and safer place to live.

"I can probably walk there myself now," she said as she attempted to pull away from him but swayed again.

Alan grabbed her firmly. "I don't think so. I'll walk you all the way home. We need to make sure you make it. Just hold on to my arm." He could not let her walk home though it was only across the street, since he would worry through the entire dinner with Missy wondering if Grace had made it or not. He needed to take her all the way up to her apartment, if just for the peace of mind knowing she was safe.

They crossed through the parking lot. The entire area was full of carts scattered here and there, and even against, numerous vehicles. Neither one thought about how strange it was to have so many vehicles in the parking lot but little to no customers to be seen coming in and out of the store.

Alan was only focused on Grace's wellbeing to notice that interesting fact.

"Damn, Peli, she never collects the carts on her shift. I don't think I've ever seen her even bring in any carts."

"Me either." Grace said and then giggled. "I haven't seen her do any work, ever."

Alan laughed in acknowledgement.

The apartment building was one of the older buildings in the area and had seen its better days. The retail space on the first floor was empty and most of the windows were boarded up at that level. Several homeless bodies were snuggled up in the crevasses of the building as they settled in for the night. As they approached the building, the fog thickened.

Grace pulled out her key but struggled to get the door unlocked. Her shirt shifted once again and revealed the emerald dragon tattoo which wrapped up the back of her neck. Alan suddenly remembered Grace's necklace that she usually wore. A green dragon on a very dainty chain. "Grace, where's your necklace?" She was not wearing it anymore. He was positive that he saw it on her earlier that day. She always wore it.

Grace stopped and touched her neck. It wasn't there. "It must have fallen off in the Booth when I fainted. I can get it tomorrow."

The fog continued to thicken as Grace struggled to get the key in the lock. Alan noticed the tattoo again, the dragon's skin seemed to glisten momentarily and for a split second he thought it moved. "That's a great tattoo," he said. "It looks like it actually moves."

Grace opened the door at that moment and stood up as she pulled her shirt to cover it. "Oh? Don't be silly. Thank you. I'm good now." She attempted to close the door on Alan, but he stuck his foot into the doorway and pushed his way in.

"Not yet. What floor is your apartment on?"

"Third."

"See, you're not home yet." He smiled and walked past her to the elevator and pushed the button.

CHAPTER 10

Dragon Spirit

The business executive who had attempted to lure Darci out from the dairy case earlier that day, peered into the front lobby from the entrance. He scanned the lobby and only saw Paul standing at the register, again reading a magazine. No one else was around, so he snuck in and headed towards the back of the store.

He cautiously looked down the aisles as he passed them to check and make sure Alan was not around. He finally reached the dairy section. He stood in front of the dairy case and looked down the aisle both ways quickly to confirm no one had seen him. He moved several cartons of milk until he could see past the dairy products and into the darkness of the dairy box itself.

"Darci? Darci, are you still back there? I told you I need you. I really do. I'd follow you to hell and back again if you wanted me to. Yes, I am married, but it's nothing to lose your head over. We can work it out. I know we can. Let me taste your creamy breasts one more time, please?"

From the back of the dairy box, something fell over. He attempted to lean further between the shelves and pushed part of his body into the back of the shelf so he could get a better look into the dairy box.

"Hello?" he asked as he waited for his eyes to adjust to the darkness. He attempted to back out from between the shelves, but his belt buckle caught on the bottom shelf railing. He was stuck. He looked forward and thought if he could slide forward a little bit that might help unlatch his belt. As he did that, he caught a glimpse of Darci's olive-colored apron and her large breasts. He smiled and reached out to caress her breasts with his hands. He twisted his body in an attempt to look up at her.

It took him a few seconds to orient himself to the angle, but then he realized Darci's head was hanging off to the side, unnaturally, and the breast which he was caressing, was not entirely attached to her body.

He immediately struggled to pull himself out from between the shelves and get away from this monstrosity. He wildly wrestled to free himself.

In the back lobby where the dairy section was located, there were no customers around to witness his predicament. But if there had been, they would have witnessed a man in a tailored suit bent over with his upper torso wedged between two dairy shelves. His body shimmied in an attempt to pull out but instead lurched forward deeper into the shelves, multiple times. The man screamed with each tug. Then, his entire body was yanked in and disappeared. The products on the shelf slid back into place and closed the hole that he was pulled through.

♦ ♦ ♦

Grace sat at a small table by the window of her apartment. She looked outside, watching closely, through the fog, the activity in the parking lot across the street. A small number of customers continued to park and walk into the store. No one was coming out. More carts were scattered among the cars. Occasionally, a cart would roll in this or that direction, as if it had a mind of its own but there was no indication of any wind.

Anyone entering Grace's apartment had the immediate feeling that they had stepped back in time, since her furniture and décor was that of the early nineteen hundreds. In fact, everything was in perfect condition and did not have the appearance of being an antique since it did not reflect any wear and tear. A collection of old-time photos were hung along most of the walls. Various dragon figurines and trinkets of all different sizes and colors were scattered among the shelves.

Alan stood by the sink in the cramped kitchen, which was a few feet away from Grace. He filled a tea kettle and placed it on the stove and turned on the burner. "I'll hang out here for a little bit if you don't mind. I've got some time to kill. I know you don't like me or care for me much, but I do care what happens to you. I want to make sure you are going to be okay." He was hoping that statement would strike a truce with her, and they would not need to go into their usual verbally attack routine.

There was a long moment of silence as Grace looked at him and then back out the window. The awkwardness made Alan look away and began to really assess the apartment. The photos caught his eye first, and then the various dragons throughout the entire apartment. He did not see one that matched the dragon he saw on her back. None of them were emerald colored. "You sure have a large collection of dragons. When did you start collecting them?" he asked with a soft tone to see if he could get her to talk and warm the icy silence in the room.

Nothing. No response. He tried again, but remembering her nickname, Dragon Lady, which the coworkers used behind her back at the store, he wondered if they knew about her collection. He always thought it was because she was ancient like a dragon. "Aren't they vicious evil creatures?" Like her, he thought, but did not verbalize.

"NO!" snapped Grace. "Ignorant boy!"

Oh, there it was. The old venomous Grace that Alan knew so well. Obviously, he thought, she was feeling herself again.

"I'm sorry. Really, I am. I shouldn't have snapped at you just then," she said.

"No. No need to apologize. Good to see you're getting your strength back." Alan's verbal response was the opposite of his internal thoughts for sure.

"Guards. That's what dragons are," she whispered while gazing off into the distance while she spoke.

"Guards?"

"Yep. Guards. Most people don't know the truth about dragons. They think of them as mythical creatures in folklore. But God actually created them."

"As guards? Dragons? To guard what?" inquired Alan. He wanted to know the extent of Grace's craziness. Maybe she had a stroke back in the Booth. He wanted to keep her talking.

"Hell Gates," She again whispered her response. In the dimly lit apartment, she seemed to be a scared little child, whispering a secret to Alan.

The lighting played tricks on Alan's eyes, making Grace look like she had less and less gray hair. Even her wrinkles seemed to have softened and faded away.

"Hell...Gates?"

"It's hard to understand or comprehend. Craziness, you might say. But it's the truth. God created dragons to keep the fallen angels from returning to our world."

The teapot whistled loudly and caused Alan to jump back from the stove. Sheer insanity for sure, he thought. The teapot had startled him, and his arm shook as he poured some tea for her and himself. Then he slowly walked over to Grace and placed her tea on the small table next to her. He sat across from her with his teacup, attempting to steady his hand as he took a sip.

"So, like a guard dog? God created dragons to guard the Gates of Hell?" asked Alan skeptically. "Why would God create gates if he didn't want them to return? I'm sure he didn't want us to go there either, did he?" Alan could not believe his own questions, feeding into her delusion. He thought he would play along and get a good laugh out of it later. Her appearance was serious the entire time. He also wanted to make sure she was not setting him up to humiliate him with some elaborate joke later.

"In case they repented their sins for defying him. He created thirteen gates which they could use to return to his Grace. Angels are powerful, so to make sure they didn't force their way back into our world, he created more powerful creatures for one purpose only – to guard the Hell Gates."

Alan was not sure how to respond. He wanted to just leave and forget everything he was hearing, but her conviction about this topic intrigued him. "Thirteen gates? How do you know there are Thirteen?"

"Were Thirteen, originally. Now there're only seven."

"Seven?"

"Yep."

Oh, Alan dreaded to ask, but he had to. Wanted to. He was still struggling in his mind about dragons being guards to the Gates of Hell, of which he was just told there were originally thirteen, but now only seven remained. Oh God forgive me, Alan thought to himself. He was not one to pray to God much, though when he was a kid living on his own, he often asked God to help him survive the nights living out on the streets. It might have only been three days out on his own after running away from his father, but he knew he would not survive if he did not ask for help, and God was the only one he knew he could ask. He did not know anyone else. God answered his prayers when the next day he was caught shoplifting, and the shop owner took him in. He figured God had to have had some play in that since most people would have called the police and hauled him off. "Ok, I have to ask – Why only seven now?"

Grace sat back in her chair and stared at him for a moment. "Are you mocking me? Do you think this is a joke?"

"No, not at all." He placed his hands on her hands and leaned forward with all sincerity. "I am genuinely interested in hearing more about this. It's just something I've never heard of before."

"Very few have. History has hidden the truth for thousands of years and so dragons faded into folklore and the imagination. Or perhaps the fallen angels themselves somehow were able to hide the truth from us so they could sneak back into our world and enslave us all."

Alan downed his tea, then sprung up and walked over to the wall, looking closely at one photo; attempting to distract his mind from the absurdity he was hearing. Most of the photos were that of one particular young Chinese girl at various locations around San Francisco. Occasionally, a mature Caucasian man, wearing a cutaway morning coat with trousers and a high-collared shirt along with gloves and a top-hat, was in the picture standing next to her. Alan guessed the photos were taken in San Francisco around the early nineteen hundreds of similar vintage as the furniture in the apartment.

Alan searched for something to say. Something to change the subject from the ridiculous topic they were just discussing. He could not think of anything. Then one of the photos of the girl standing on a cable car startled him. She wore the same dress that the Asian lady wore on the subway train from his dreams last night. He stepped backwards and literally fell back into the chair.

"I like you, Alan. In fact, I admire how everyone immediately likes you from the first time they get introduced to you and think you are a great guy. It all comes so naturally for you. I have to work at it, most people don't like me." She continued to speak, but in a peculiar trance tone, as she remained fixated on the grocery store. "You could go anywhere, see anything in the world, and yet you stay here at this old store for all these years while your youth escapes you. You are capable of so much more, but yet you settle on staying here."

Alan remained silent as Grace talked. He wondered if she was talking about him or herself. It seemed more of a profound emotional reflection of oneself, so he didn't think she was actually talking about him. Possibly she had regrets herself about working all these years at the store. He left to get the teapot.

"Things come so easy for you and you barely apply yourself. You should go out and experience the world and see where your potential takes you. Live life to the fullest. Thank you," she said as he returned and refilled their cups. He turned around and taking a few steps, placed it back on the stove and returned to his seat.

As he picked up his cup to take a sip, he noticed the picture frame on the table which contained the same young Chinese woman from the photos on the wall. This time though she was dressed in a traditional Chinese embroidered silk dress. Next to her was the same older gentleman as they posed on the San Francisco pier. A boat in the background showed passengers disembarking. Alan picked up the frame and looked at it more closely. "Who is she? She's so beautiful, even in a black and white photo. Is this your mother or grandmother?"

When Alan grabbed the frame and took it from the table, Grace snapped out of her trance and she leaned towards him, staring intensely into his eyes while grabbing his hands, but then paused. She relaxed her grip on him and sat back, then bashfully looked away.

"I will deny I ever said this to you, but that's me. It was April 17th, 1906. I had just arrived in San Francisco with my father. It was a charming Spring day."

"You're kidding, right? You couldn't be over a hundred years old? Good Joke. Really, who is she?"

"No joke," she said as she reached across the table and softly touched his arm. Her eyes pleaded with him to believe her. "Believe it or not, but I am over a hundred years old. But, like any proper lady would do, I'd deny it."

"No way. You're obviously old, but not that old. I meant, why would you still be working? Shouldn't you have retired by now?"

"I have to work. How else do I pay for this little piece of paradise with this magnificent view of Tony's just outside my window? I can't go anywhere."

"I thought you said you were Dutch. Looks more like you came over on a boat from China," commented Alan, as he pointed to the photo and particularly pointed at the outfit she was wearing. "And I mean no disrespect either. Seriously I don't."

"I am Dutch. My father and mother were from Holland. They traveled a lot since he was a scientist. He took us everywhere with him. My mother passed away before my first birthday. He'd never leave me alone with relatives or friends. We came to San Francisco because of a dream he had."

"So, he came here to see his dream come true. That's awesome."

Grace did not comment on his enthusiastic statement as she played with her teacup while lost in a memory of many years ago. "No, actually he died the next morning in the earthquake. Buildings collapsed around us and the fire-fiend, I meant the fires, were like a fire-fiend burning everything in sight. I am not sure how I survived it."

The more he learned about Grace and her past, the harder it was to keep up that wall against liking her and feeling sorry for her. What a tough life she must have suffered, losing her father on the second day here in a new country and on the other side of the world from everything she knew. "I'm sorry. I didn't mean to bring up any terrible memories. It must be very painful still." He noticed tears started to fill her eyes and she stayed locked onto his eyes for the longest time. He felt she was building up the courage to unload years of bottled-up emotions at any moment. The tea kettle whistled from the kitchen and Alan stood up and rushed into the kitchen. "Oops. Forgot to turn off the stove. Be right back."

◆ ◆ ◆

The produce section on the main floor of the store was completely empty of customers. There were several abandoned grocery carts, but no signs of any customers.

The punk that challenged Alan earlier that day walked through the produce area carrying a twelve pack of beer. He stopped next to the front bins where the pistachios and artichokes were displayed. He scanned the area and being confident no one was around to see him, he reached down and swiped up a handful of pistachios. He quickly threw them back down into the bin. "What the fuck!?" he exclaimed as he examined his bloody hand.

There were many tiny bite marks all over his hand. He looked down at the pistachio bin and all the nuts were snapping open and closed like little mouths. The nuts that he threw back into the bin now had red shells instead of their natural beige coloring. He could not believe what he was witnessing and backed up into the other bin behind him. He spun around in fear it was another bin of pistachios, but it was a full stack of artichokes. The punk laughed at himself. He remembered he had taken some of his friend's pills before he left for the store to get beer. What a bad trip he was experiencing, he thought. He then bent over the artichokes to examine them closely. "Do you guys move too?" He said jokingly.

The entire artichoke bin opened their leaves and revealed their internal purple flower to him. They did this a couple of times and then several artichokes shot their tiny thorns into his face and blinded him. He screamed and attempted to cover his face as he stumbled back and fell on top of the pistachio bin. Like piranhas, the little nuts devoured his entire body almost instantly. His arm reached up and out for help, but no one came to his rescue. His feet were the last to disappear down into the bin.

♦ ♦ ♦

Alan and Grace sat at the small table and both just stared out the window while they sipped tea. He would occasionally look over at her. Alan was beginning to see Grace as a real person and perhaps that is why he did not think much of the fact that her wrinkles seemed to be diminishing. Her ancient scowl was softening he thought; even her hands and fingers did not seem as boney as before. He even noticed more black streaks in her hair that he had not noticed before. He was amazed how someone's appearance changed so much just based on how you felt about them. "Feeling better? You're looking much better." The green dragon tattoo slithered round her neck for a moment then froze into a different position. Alan had noticed it but did not say anything. He had heard and seen enough for one night and did not want to know why her tattoo seemed to come alive on her body.

"Yes, I believe I am. Thank you. I'm sorry for being so nasty to you lately. I'd like to say it was hormonal, but you know that hasn't occurred for a long time." She quietly giggled and returned to staring out the window and sipping her tea.

Alan was curious about that dragon around her neck. He knew it moved and it was not his imagination. He looked around the room trying to find some way to bring it up naturally.

Alan's cell phone rang at that moment and caused both of them to jump from the sound. Alan fumbled through his pockets, trying to find his phone. He took it out and answered it. "Missy, hey what's up? We're still on, right? What? I am? That's not possible. I just dropped Grace off at her apartment about 20 minutes ago around seven pm. It's 8:10 now?" Alan searched the room for a clock and finally found one on the end table next to the couch. It was old and had elaborate filigree arms on it. It was 8:10. "Crap! I'm sorry. Don't go anywhere. I'm on my way. Please, wait."

He hung up and slipped the phone back into his shirt pocket as he headed out of her apartment. As he opened the door, he turned back around towards Grace. "I'm late for my date. I must go. You look great so you'll be fine. Call my cell if you need anything. Seriously, I mean it, call me if you need anything. Bye." He slipped out the door, flew down the stairs, bypassing the elevator all together, and disappeared into the fog.

Grace stared at the door for a long time. There was so much more she wanted to tell him. She had not shared any of her father's work in all these years before now and worried that it might scare Alan off. Why now, she thought. Why share that information with this young man who was too scared to explore the real world and was satisfied with just existing at this store. Why would he be willing to accept the fact that there were Gates throughout the world which could allow anything from Hell to pass into their world.

It was foolish for her to even think that way. She was alone on this journey, since her father was gone, and she did not know anyone else who would believe her. She not only knew about the Gate beneath the store, but she also felt it was about to open again. She wondered if she was strong enough to stop it one more time. The dragon spirit had been awakened and she needed to find out who or what was responsible.

CHAPTER 11

Alan's Revelation

Alan ran out of Grace's apartment building and looked back at the Food Mart where his car was parked under the neon sign. He heard the bell ringing on an approaching trolley car and it soon flew by him.

The decision was easy to make. He ran after the trolley and jumped aboard. He clung to the bar on the side of the trolley. His mind was racing with so many different thoughts. He could not believe he was late to see Missy. He could not believe what he had just experienced in Grace's apartment. Images of Grace, the young Asian lady on the subway from his dream, and the emerald dragon on her back and...Oh my God! Alan thought. He just then remembered the green dragon in his dream. All the images bombarded his mind so fast that he almost lost his grip and fell off the trolley car. He shook his head back and forth for a moment to clear his mind.

At the intersection of Powell and California Street, the cable car slowed down. Alan jumped off. He dashed across the street to Vinnie's Restaurant. He looked through the windows frantically searching for Missy, hoping she was still waiting for him inside. As he approached the entrance, he noticed a woman walking away from the restaurant. He knew that walk as he had watched it many times in the store. It was Missy.

"Missy! Where are you going?" he yelled after her. She paused for a second mid-stride, but then continued walking. She did not even look back at him. Alan ran after her. "I still have forty minutes of my dinner break."

She stopped, turned around, and watched him approach. Her face was stern and non-emotional. "Just forget it. It was a mistake. I don't know why I agreed to meet with you." She then continued on her path to her banged up, faded blue Smart car.

He reached out to grab her arm to stop her from opening her car door, but in doing so, he knocked her purse off her shoulder which caused several items to spill out onto the street. "Oh God! I'm sorry. I didn't mean to do that." He bent down and picked up the contents and attempted to put them back into her purse.

Missy kneeled herself and tried to gather up what she could very quickly. She pushed his hands away from her stuff. "I can do it! Really, just leave me alone."

He grabbed a bottle of pills and noticed they were a prescription. He handed them back to her as she snatched them from him and buried them in the bottom of her purse. "I'm sorry, really I am. Don't be embarrassed about the pills."

"What?"

Alan pointed to her purse. "The sleeping pills. I've seen those pills before. Paul uses them when he has anxiety the night before a game and can't sleep. They knock him right out. It's nothing to be ashamed of. We all need help occasionally."

He picked up the few remaining items and handed them to her. She grabbed her car keys. The last thing Alan picked up was a credit card and he noticed the name printed on it—Harry M. Buggee. He handed it back to her.

"I'd prefer it if you would leave now and never talk to me or look at me again. I don't exist, at least not in your world." She ripped the credit card from Alan's hand and turned to unlock her car.

"Who's Harry?" asked Alan.

That statement stopped Missy in her tracks, and she turned back around to face him, moving into his personal space threateningly. "You read my credit card? Really? What? Now you're stalking me? Really? That's my first name. My father wanted a boy desperately. That's why I go by my middle name. I don't have to explain myself to you." She jumped into her car and drove off.

Alan stood alone on the sidewalk under a streetlamp. The deserted street and slight fog hanging about added a nip of chilliness to the air, which only added to the heaviness he felt at that moment. Alan walked along the sidewalk back towards Tony's Food Mart, back to where he had picked up the cable car. He disappeared into the fog. It thickened as he descended the hill.

◆ ◆ ◆

Mr. Greyson looked through the remaining donuts that were left on the tray on the top of the bakery case. The case had a sign stating they were fifty percent off. He assessed them closely, debating which ones he would select. He wanted to choose the most sugary and unhealthy ones, so when he went through Mandy's lane again, like he had done earlier in the day, she would verbally abuse him. He heard someone giggle behind him. He turned around and saw a short person sneak behind the bakery case and disappear. He heard the giggle again.

"Mandy? Is that you? I'd know that giggle anywhere." He sneaked over to the side of the bakery case and bent down to peek around the corner. No one was there.

While Mr. Greyson was bent over, the Lemure-possessed Baker Bob statue shoved a long thin baguette into his buttocks, impaling him. Mr. Greyson's eyes widened as he inhaled instinctively and smiled, but then the bloody baguette shot out of his mouth.

In the back of the Bakery Department, Bill hung his apron on a coat hook on the wall, then he turned off the lights in the back room. The side door in the bakery led to the parking lot, so he opened the door to leave. Suddenly, he heard the large mixing machine turn on. He came back into the building and turned the lights back on.

He approached the large mixer and saw that it was full of blood and various parts of Mr. Greyson's flesh. Then the bread slicer started up and Bill looked over to witness it slicing Mr. Greyson's head.

"What the hell!?" exclaimed Bill, as he slowly backed up towards the side door.

There was a giggle behind him, and Bill saw a small baker hat pop up on the other side of the large wooden baking table, but then it disappeared. He walked around the table to see where the hat had disappeared to, but the lights turned off and the area darkened instantly.

"Shit, where's that switch?" He reached over to the wall as he felt around for it in the dark. The lights turned back on and Bill turned towards the side door to run, but just as he was about to lift his leg, he noticed that spread over the entire baking table were body parts. Bill stumbled backwards and almost fell into the mixer himself.

The giggle returned, but this time it had a much more sinister sound to it. Baker Bob jumped up onto the table and sprinted at Bill while swinging a rolling pin.

"Time to bake from scratch again, dough boy!" wickedly laughed Baker Bob as he clobbered Bill on the side of his head.

♦ ♦ ♦

The street was murky with a heavy fog. The illumination of the streetlamps created a little dotted line like crumbs along a trail. Alan walked alone and followed the trail to keep himself on the right path. The fog concealed others that passed by him, though he could hear their steps approach and then disappear. His mind was in deep thought, focused on Missy and himself, but not about what had just happened. Nope. It was about what happened two weeks ago. He was recalling memories, mixed with thoughts of what might really have occurred that night. What is up with these crazy women? He thought to himself. What the hell did I do wrong that night? Come on Alan, why can't you remember? I wasn't that drunk. I only had one drink. He asked himself over and over though not really expecting to actually answer himself. He was attempting to pull back details from that night at the restaurant. There were gaps surrounding his memories, but why? These gaps seemed thicker than the fog in which he was currently walking.

She was the one who approached him at the bar, with that big, friendly, toothy smile, and handed him a drink. He had showed up early that evening to wait for a bunch of coworkers that were getting off work soon. They were going to throw some darts and just hang out. She showed up before the others and said they were on their way. But he did not remember anyone else ever showing up. They drank and small talked about who had the craziest customer that day. She laughed and touched his arm and shoulder a couple of times while he continued with his story. Next, there was a glass being handed to him. He took a sip of it and everything went black again.

The next thing he remembered was that he drove her to his place. No. Wait. She drove him there, in his car. Why can't I remember getting to my apartment? It's all a blank. This lapse in memory was really beginning to concern Alan since he had never been drunk enough to black out. Something was not right here. He continued to ponder the possibilities and an explanation.

His next memory was that of sitting on the edge of his bed while Missy stood next to his dresser, making drinks for them. Her purse was on the dresser next to her. She pulled something out of it, a bottle of pills. No, that can't be, he thought. I just saw those same pills tonight. I must be imagining it.

Alan then remembered opening his eyes and realizing he was under the sheets in his bed, stripped down to his boxers. He looked over towards the bathroom and saw Missy's reflection in the mirror. She appeared to be talking on her cell phone. His clothes were on the chair next to the bathroom door and his work keys were clipped to the side of his belt. No, his keys were not there, though he knew they were always attached to his belt. That is odd, where were they? Then another blank.

Alan remembered no other details from that night and his memories picked up the next morning when he woke up late for his trip to Sacramento for Management Training. Missy was gone. His keys were gone. No, they were there again, attached to his belt on the chair. Why were his memories so jumbled up? It did not make any sense-none of it made any sense.

Alan stopped on the corner next to Grace's apartment building. He pulled out his keys to examine them more closely. That Bitch took my work keys! These aren't mine. No wonder I couldn't open the Booth door tonight. But why would Missy do that? He bounced those thoughts around in his head and tried to understand what her motives could be.

He threw the fake work keys on the ground. The crosswalk lights were still red. Normally he would just jaywalk across the street, but he knew better because of the heaviness of the fog and low visibility. He did not want to get hit by a car or even worse, a cable car. They might make a lot of noise, but in the fog, you did not always know from which direction they were coming.

A short figure suddenly appeared next to him out of the fog and waited to cross the street as well. The person seemed to appear out of thin air and took him by surprise. The fog could easily play tricks on your mind. He did not feel threatened by the person, just nervous because he did not know how long they had been next to him. He looked down at the shadowy person who was wearing a hooded jacket. Though he could not see the person's face, he did get a quick glimpse of a glistening emerald dragon tattoo on the person's neckline.

"Grace?" He asked, but the person did not look up at him when he asked the question.

After a long moment of silence, she responded. "Yes, Alan. It's me. I'm feeling much better and wanted to finish the accounting reports tonight." She never looked at him when she spoke, so he could not see her face.

"Okay. But don't push yourself. Even though you don't think so, you are fragile. You need to know your limits. You're not getting any younger."

"Like the limits you place on yourself? What happened to your date?"

The traffic lights finally changed, and they crossed the street together. Grace walked at a faster pace to keep just ahead of him.

"You were right, as always, I'm bad at profiling. She wanted me for something else."

CHAPTER 12

Grace's Confession

The two crossed the street and headed towards the front entrance of the store. There were a variety of vehicles parked throughout the parking lot. Alan paused for a second and stared at a car that looked exactly the same as the one Missy had driven away from the restaurant.

"Interesting. This is Missy's car. Why would she come back here this late at night?"

"Maybe to apologize?" Grace responded, skeptically.

They continued walking to the front entrance and passed a substantial number of grocery carts haphazardly scattered throughout the lot.

They entered the store without passing one customer the entire time. Grace darted off to the booth and Alan was almost run over by Mrs. Murphy's cart as she barreled passed him and out the store doors.

"Excuse me, Mrs. Murphy. I told you to stop running people over on purpose. I just might decide to run you over one day to see how you like it." Alan could not believe he just said that to a customer. His face flushed red as he had never addressed a customer like that before. He thought of it many of times but could never bring himself to respond that way.

"What a rude young man you are! If I wasn't in such a hurry, I'd tell your manager. In fact, I will tell him tomorrow morning when I come back in."

Alan just stared at this sweet, self-centered, old, batty woman and imagined the other customers ramming into her and then groping her but he stopped instantly when he realized that she would probably enjoy it. He turned his attention to Grace to make sure she could make it to the booth. She made it to the booth just fine on her own and without his help.

Mrs. Murphy continued out of the store, headed towards her classic, white and black-trimmed, 1959 Oldsmobile Ninety-Eight. As she walked pushing the cart, her it shook when she ran over a gooey Lemure. For a brief moment she could not push or pull the cart in either direction. She looked down at the wheels and saw only a small glob of jelly-like residue. She tried to push the cart again and walked with it until it bumped into the side of her own car. She parked the cart against the side of the car's back fender and walked around to the trunk and tried to unlock it but was unsuccessful.

The cart rolled away from the car momentarily, then turned back towards her.

Frustrated that she could not open the trunk, Mrs. Murphy took a step backwards and bumped into the cart. "Oh dear. How'd you roll over here?" She grabbed the cart and pushed it again up to the rear bumper. She again tried to unlock the trunk. A different cart slammed into the bumper on the other side of where she was standing. Being startled, Mrs. Murphy turned and fell to the ground, pinned between the two carts and the back of her car. Her head rested on the silvery, steel rear bumper. A third cart flew in between the other two carts. It lined up for a direct hit to her head against the bumper. Her head exploded like a ripe watermelon.

In the front lobby of the store Mandy stood at the register, reading some type of healthy food magazine.

"Has it been busy while I was gone?" asked Alan. It irritated him when he saw lazy Checkers standing around when they could be helping to straighten up the front displays of each aisle. But no. Instead, they just stood there and read magazines.

"I thought it was going to be busy since I saw a lot of people come in, but no one has come up to the registers yet. Mrs. Murphy was like the first customer out the door in the last twenty minutes. I called Paul to relieve me so I can go home, but as you can see, no show yet."

"It's after nine p.m., so it's closing time. Make the announcement and I'll turn off the door sensors so they won't open for new customers walking up, wanting to come in. I don't have my keys to lock them now, but I'll look for the spare set in the Booth in a sec. "Has night crew come in yet? Where's Missy?"

"Haven't seen either yet." Mandy said as she pulled her phone off the hook and started to speak into it. "Attention Tony's Food Mart customers. We are now closed. Please bring all your final purchases up to the register now. Thank you and have a good evening." The message echoed over the paging system.

As Mandy was paging, Alan walked over to the front of the store and reached up in the top center of the sliding doors and flipped the power switch off. The doors slowly closed. He pressed his face up against the glass, attempting to look out into the parking lot to see if any customers were approaching. But the fog allowed only a few feet of visibility into outside world. He could see just to the end of the sidewalk.

"Oh wait! I think I saw Mike down one of the aisles talking to a customer when I returned from my break a while ago, after I relieved Paul for his break. So, Mike must be around here somewhere," Mandy rattled off to Alan.

"Grace," Alan yelled towards the Booth. "I need to go find Paul or Mike so they can relieve Mandy from the register. She needs to punch out for the evening. Then, I'll come back and help you close the books. I don't want you working late into the night. I will walk you back home. I wouldn't want you collapsing again."

"She collapsed? I didn't know that. Tell her to eat an apple or banana, or maybe some almonds. It will keep her old body energized," remarked Mandy as she returned to reading the magazine.

Alan headed towards the Produce Department and in frustration stared at Mandy as he passed her register. "Really, reading a magazine again? Straighten up the candy or gum or something."

"You're as bad as Mr. Helovich. Always wanting us to work every second. Relaxation is good for you and so is reading." She grumbled as she dropped the magazine on the counter, stepped over to the gum display and acted like she was organizing it, as she stared back at him.

Alan power-walked towards the back of the store. As he approached the produce section, he noticed the pistachio bin, which now had red shells, no longer beige ones, and skeletal remains mixed in with the nuts. The bones were picked clean of any flesh. The artichoke bin was full, and he noticed, how they were stacked facing the pistachio bin, not towards the front of the store.

Alan stopped for a moment and assessed the two promotional bins. The pistachio shells were never red, he thought. The bones must be some early Halloween prank.

The little nuts chattered, then turned towards Alan snapping their shells for more blood. The artichokes opened wide and revealed their deep purple centers to him. Several thorns shot out and embedded themselves into his name tag.

"Shit!" exclaimed Alan, jumping back and scrambling to the front lobby. The artichokes shot several more thorns at him, but they flew by embedding in various items along the shelves next to him.

Alan, headed towards the front doors, ran past Mandy who was reading the health magazine again at her register. "Get the hell out of here, Mandy, now!"

Alan reached the front doors, but stopped, realizing that he had to manually open them, since he had turned off the power. Suddenly, the doors opened on their own and a grocery cart flew into the store.

Avoiding colliding with the cart, Alan dodged back towards the register. He saw Mrs. Murphy's mangled body in the cart as it traveled beyond him and down the aisle towards the back room.

"Was that Mrs. Murphy?" questioned Mandy. "That's not real, right?"

Alan stumbled over to Mandy's register and rested his entire body on it, trying to hold himself up. The cart had clipped him harder than he originally thought. He looked at Mandy to respond but noticed several red laser beams from the register's scanner reflected off Mandy's apron. The beams continued to move back and forth as they traveled across her chest and then up her neck. She noticed Alan's eyes following up her body. She looked down and noticed the light on her also. "That's strange," she commented.

Why the hell is the scanner doing that? pondered Alan.

As the beams reached her neck, they joined into one light source and sliced across her neck. Mandy's head rolled off her body and dropped onto the counter. Her head landed so that it faced Alan and her eyes moved and looked directly into his eyes. Her mouth continued to move, but no sound came out.

"Fuck, I'm out of here! Grace, we need to leave now," screamed Alan, hoping she would come running out of the Booth immediately, but nothing happened. He moved towards the front doors which had shut automatically after the cart with Mrs. Murphy's body in it shot by him. He attempted to open the doors again. "Grace! Now! We have to go!"

"What's wrong," responded Grace.

"Please move your ass! Hello? I'm not kidding!" Alan attempted to slide one of the doors then the other one, but neither would budge.

Grace screamed. She stood next to the express register, staring at Mandy's head on the counter.

Alan turned around to face her. "Forgot to warn you about that. Sorry," he said, as his eyes were apparently playing a trick on him. Perhaps he was just in a dream again. Before him was not the old Grace he knew, but the young woman from the old-time photos in Grace's apartment. Also, the young lady on the train in his dream. This must be a dream, he thought. "Who the hell are you?" he asked. But then he saw the green dragon tattoo around her neck. "Grace?"

"Yep. It's a long story."

"You can tell me later. We need to get out of here." He grabbed her hand and pushed again on one of the doors. It began to open, but then a cart crashed into the glass door. Then another cart and another. He let go of the door and it closed.

Who the hell was pushing the carts into the door? More and more carts now rolled up to the front of the store. no one was pushing them. They apparently just seemed to have minds of their own. Alan turned to Grace, noticing that he was still holding tightly onto her hand.

"I need to explain something to you, Alan."

He released her hand and took a couple steps back away from her. "Explain what? This isn't going to be good news, is it?" He asked cautiously as his mind was catching up with all the stuff he had just experienced in such a short time frame.

His brain was trying to piece together the facts, to make some coherent sense of it all. Most of what he witnessed was impossible, so he attempted to try to associate what he experienced with any horror movie he had ever watched. Run, run away fast, was what his instinct was telling him. The people that did not listen to their instinct in horror movies always ended up dead. He did not want to be one of them.

"I don't want to freak you out or sound crazy, but..."

"You don't think I'm a little freaked out right now? I just saw Mrs. Murphy's twisted body in a cart zoom by me, mind you, with no one pushing it. Man-eating pistachios. Artichokes that shoot thorns at you. Oh, and that scanner just cut off Mandy's head. I'm sure whatever you have to share with me isn't going to freak me out any more than I already am!"

"Calm down. I can't explain it if you're not listening."

"There are carts knocking at the front door on their own. Does that sound crazy? What crazier thing can you tell me than that? Perhaps you're a demon, sucking everyone's soul so you can be young again?

"What did you say?"

"Oh, my God! It's true. You are a demon. You're going to suck my soul out of me, aren't you?" Alan continued to back up towards the Front Booth. He then turned around and ran into the Booth, slamming the door behind him before Grace could enter.

"Alan! Open the door! Let me explain. Let me in." She pounded on the door. "You know the lock is broken on the door, right? Remember, you broke it."

Alan pushed against the door with his body weight, while he grabbed whatever he could to wedge it against the door. "Explain it to me but while you're out there."

The front doors of the store opened, and carts cruised in from the outside. Some carts even rolled up from the aisleways and into the front lobby.

"Ah, Alan?" she pounded harder on the door. "Let me in now! The front door just opened, and the carts are coming in. Alan!

He looked out the one-way glass and saw the carts rolling into the store. They seem to be searching for something as they all went in their own direction. "You will just need to explain it a little faster now, okay? I'm not letting any sexy young Dutch demon suck out my soul without an explanation."

"You're ridiculous!"

"I'm ridiculous? I'm not 100 years old, parading around like some twenty-year-old." He looked out again through the one-way glass and did not see Grace standing outside anymore. "Grace? You're standing behind me, aren't you?"

"Yep, how d'you know?" she stood on the counter looking down at him.

"What else would a demon do but fly up and over the top, since there's no fucking roof on this stupid room."

"I'm NOT a demon! And I didn't fly, I jumped over."" She hopped down off the counter. "Don't be so childish!"

Alan backed up and was almost out the door.

"Don't go out there! I'll stay in one spot. Just keep the door shut and be quiet. It will take a while for the Lemures to find us if we're quiet."

"Lemurs? Like in monkeys?"

"Ssh. I'll explain, but first, did you leave the safe open when you took me home?"

"No. I closed it and spun the dial like you trained me to do whenever you leave the Booth. Need to make sure I secure it whenever leaving the Booth. Always. The door lock was broken so I put all the cash into the safe before we left. Why?"

"It's empty," she said as she pointed to the safe. The door was wide open. "Nothing there. Mr. Helovich would not have taken it either. This is the only safe we have in the store. We've been robbed."

"What would 'Lemur' monkeys want with cash? What would they do with it? And wouldn't they have left by now?"

Grace's face contorted into a sour expression as she shook her head. "Lemures don't need cash. They are pawns for a powerful fallen angel. His name is Samael. He was the one who broke through the Gate back in 1906. Someone else robbed the store after we left."

"Fallen Angels? Samael? Lemures? What in the world are you talking about? This is so ridiculous. Let's call 9-1-1." He picked up the phone, but it was dead. No dial tone. Alan then pulled out his cell phone to call, but no luck. It showed no signal found. "No signal. Really? I've always had a signal in this store before. Even in the basement."

"Please believe me. How would you explain my appearance? Those carts out there driving themselves around? I'd like to hear your explanation, but if you don't have one, then let me talk."

"I don't have one. I can't think of anything logical at the moment."

"So, listen to me then. One of the Hell Gates is about to open and I need to help the Dragon Spirit to stop that from happening. It needs to borrow a human soul and bind with it so it can take on a physical form and fight Samael once he breaks through."

"One of the Hell Gates? Here in this store? Seriously. So, there really are thirteen Hell Gates? I mean seven?"

"Not in the store. The Gate is under the store. As I told you before there were thirteen Gates originally, but six were permanently sealed by a Gold Dragon Spirit. Those Gates are permanently closed and cannot be reopened by man or angel. Fallen or not."

A cart slammed into the Booth door. And then another.

"They know where we are. We need to get out of here," said Grace.

"There's a side door in the Bakery Department. We can get out that way." Alan was still unsure about all of this and what she was saying, but it was the only explanation that could make sense, if you could stretch your brain enough.

"I told you I can't leave. I must stop this from occurring again. Samael almost escaped last time. My father bound together with the Dragon Spirit and formed a sapphire Dragon. The fight was epic and shook the entire city. It was not an earthquake that day. The Blue Dragon's power is electricity. Samael appeared to know that fact and easily deflected the attacks. He killed my father. Samael started to walk away from the Gate in his fiery fiend form towards the downtown area.

So, the Blue Dragon spirit searched for another soul. It found me and bound with me. When it did that, it could take on the form of a new type of dragon, an emerald one, whose power is that of acidic toxic gas. It was able to force Samael back through the gate. I am its sentinel now, and we will be united to fight Samael again when he passes through that Gate. We are bound together for eternity. That's why I'm young again. The Dragon Spirit was awoken by a new threat, which is attempting to force open the Gate by loosening the Dragon's seal over it."

There was another loud crash on the door as a speeding cart slammed into it and shattered the one-way mirror in the middle of the door.

"Ok," spit out Alan as he attempted to catch his breath from the shock of the last impact to the door. "Whatever you say, but let's get out of here."

The store lights flickered and then went out. Then, back on. A couple seconds later, the lights were back off again.

When the lights returned, Ms. Pepper was standing directly in front of the Customer Service Window staring in at Grace and Alan. Her vivid red and orange hair looked like long streaming flames. Her makeup matched it, as did her pantsuit in reds and oranges. "Did you two lose something?" she asked, and then roared with a sinister laugh. The lights went out again.

Alan moved back towards Grace so he could stand next to her. The lights came back on. Grace jumped slightly, as Alan was now only inches away from her. Then they both noticed Ms. Pepper's head sat directly in front of them on the counter. "You lost your heads!" She delivered her punchline and literally laughed her head off.

Grace's immediate reaction was to grab the head by its long flaming hair and fling it, with all her might, over the booth wall, as far away from them as possible. Ms. Pepper's headless body then ran off in the same direction as its head had flown.

"We're going to need flashlights before going down into the basement. Aisle 4?"

"Nope. Manager's office," replied Alan. "I'm not even going to try going down one of those aisles to get a flashlight and then try to get over to the battery aisle. Not with those roaming, possessed carts out there."

Grace climbed back up onto the counter. "Let's get out of here." She reached down to Alan for his hand so she could pull him up, but he brushed her hand to the side and climbed up himself.

"We can circle around the perimeter of the outer store wall by cutting through the Bakery Department. There's a door at the back that opens onto the back lobby which is also kiddie-corner to the Meat Department door. It will keep us off the main floor, avoiding the carts in the aisles."

Alan climbed over the top of the booth wall and slipped down behind a floor display. He waited for Grace to climb over, but noticed she was immediately standing behind him as she had just leaped high into the air, did a twisted flip, and landed on both feet.

"Perks of having the powers of a dragon running through you. I'm getting stronger also," she bragged.

Alan and Grace kneeled behind a bakery table as carts patrolled the area. The store lights continued to randomly flicker off and on throughout each section of the store. Baker Bob was missing from the front display case of the Bakery area. The only thing that remained was his base and the sign listing the daily specials.

"Someone stole Baker Bob. I can't believe they not only stole our cash but Baker Bob too!"

"Who?"

"The statue that held our daily specials. He's gone."

"You gave him a name? Bill probably put him in the back for the night. Let's move before the carts realize we're over here."

Alan and Grace crawled into the back room of the Bakery. The lights were off. On the far wall, past the oven and giant mixer, was the side door to exit the store and escape to freedom, away from whatever these creatures were that roamed the store. He sprinted to the door and Grace followed. He opened it and looked around outside. No carts. His car was just four rows away. He figured they could easily make a run for it.

"Let's get out of here, regroup, and figure out what we're dealing with."

"I can't. I must help the Dragon Spirit keep the Gate closed and stop Samael from returning to our world. Have you not been listening to me? Go save yourself. I don't have a choice. I must do this for my father. It's an honor to be a Dragon Sentinel."

"Is that why you never left? Because of the death of your father? I think he would want you to live and run from this as fast as you could. The Dragon thing can find another soul to mate with."

"You're correct, I have a choice, but this is what I choose. You have a choice too. Explore the world, something which I cannot do. Live it to the fullest every day. I am sorry. I can't be there to see it myself."

Alan scanned the parking lot again and it was still clear for them to escape. He somewhat casually strolled back into the store. "I don't believe in the sacrifice of one to save the millions or whatever that stupid saying is, but I can't let you do this alone." He then grabbed Grace and threw her over his shoulder and ran for the door. "You'll thank me later."

Grace attempted to free herself from his grip, but surprised he was much stronger than she had expected.

Alan pushed the door open but then stopped dead in his tracks, just over the threshold he faced a bunch of carts now surrounding the outside of the door. The carts slowly moved forward and then increasing in speed, rolled towards them. Alan jumped back into the store, with Grace in his arms, and slammed the door shut with his foot just before any of the carts could hit him.

He stumbled to the ground and Grace rolled off him and onto the floor as well. The lights flickered in their area. "Stupid move," he mumbled to himself.

"You think?" asked Grace sarcastically as she picked herself up off the floor. She then punched him in the shoulder.

"Ouch. I like the old Grace better. At least she didn't physically abuse me."

"Get used to it. She ain't coming back."

"Ain't? That's not perfect English. Are you a teenager now? Are you going to turn into a toddler next?

"Shut up. We need to get to the basement to stop Samael. The Gate below us." Grace turned around and the flickering light revealed Baker Bob standing on the center of the wooden prep table. Bill's head and Mr. Greyson's partial sliced head were on either side of Bob, facing them, while their body parts were spread out on cookie sheets.

"Baker Bob?" asked Alan in disbelief.

"The statue is possessed by a Lemure. Be careful."

A strange deep voice came out of Baker Bob as he stared them both down with a devilish grin. "Monkey bread time and you two are my last ingredients!"

He sprung through the air at Grace swinging his rolling pin in an attempt to hit her. Alan pushed her away as the rolling pin struck him instead. The blow stunned Alan. He stumbled to the floor, landing on his ass. Baker Bob hit the wall hard and ricocheted off it and onto the ground, ending up on his back.

Grace ran around to the other side of the table. "Alan? Alan, are you okay?" She saw the top of the chef hat pop up just beyond the edge of the table. It headed around the table after her.

Baker Bob's sinister laughter actually echoed in her mind. She ran around the table in the opposite direction to get away. She grabbed a large bread knife stuck in the table, upright, that was alongside bloody body parts. Her eyes targeted the chef's hat, and she held the knife up in front of her keeping it between herself and the hat, expecting Baker Bob to come around the corner at any second.

Grace continued to step backwards away from the table but Baker Bob was nowhere to be seen. The hat just stopped moving and paused. His laughter stopped also. Silence.

The walk-in oven doors began to open behind her, as she unknowingly backed up towards them.

Baker Bob's laughter resumed and Grace drew up the knife in response to the awful sound.

She looked down at the floor on the side where Alan had fallen. With the flickering lights, it took her a moment to realize he was not there.

"Alan? Where are you?" she whispered.

Baker Bob sprang up onto the corner of the table and sprinted right for her, brandishing his rolling pin high over his head. He had left his hat on the other side of the table as a distraction. He flew off the table directly towards her and by now the oven doors were completely open. The inside of the oven burst into flames and the room lit up.

Although everything was happening so fast around Grace, she thought how strange it was that time appeared to be slowing down. She saw Baker Bob's wicked smile as he flew towards her. She saw the room light up from some source behind her, so she turned around. The heat from the flames in the oven blasted out towards her. A hand grabbed her arm and tugged her down to the ground. As she fell, she saw Baker Bob fly over the top of her head and into the oven. Time seemed to slow down for Grace as she was motionless on the ground, but saw Alan stand up, heard the slamming of the oven doors, and finally she saw him lock the doors. Her senses calmed and time returned to normal around her.

Alan looked through the oven's window and saw Baker Bob partially on fire and running in circles, banging his rolling pin against the door. The high-pitched scream of Baker Bob pierced their ears so painfully that they had to cover them.

Alan turned to Grace and offered his hand to help her up. "Come on. We have a date with Samael," he said.

Grace reached for his outstretched hand and pulled herself up. "I may look young, but this body doesn't feel young right now," she remarked, as she rubbed several sore areas of her body.

"Let's go back up front and see if we can find an easier way to the basement. We will have to go through the Meat Department if we continue this way. I only suggested this way because I knew we could have slipped out the emergency door. I've seen enough horror movies to know that the Meat Department is the last place we should go when there are demons and devils running around."

"What do you mean? It's the only way to go to avoid the patrolling carts in the aisles and remember, we need flashlights."

"Haven't you watched any horror movies? If these Lemures can animate Baker Bob into a psycho-killer doughboy, and he's only made out of cloth, Styrofoam, and wood, then what the hell is waiting for us in the Meat Department with all of those cut-up animal parts? There are hooks and big knives and a bandsaw too. Customers' bodies are probably hanging on the hooks in the meat box, which we also have to walk through. I'm not going that direction."

"Actually, that's probably the safest place in the store. They hate animal flesh and blood. They want humans."

Alan did not like that response, but he had nothing–no facts of any kind to argue against it. Obviously, Grace had more experience than him in this area. "I'm going to have to trust you on this one, but I still think it's a bad idea."

They continued to the far back corner of the bakery and eventually reached the bakery doors which led out onto the back lobby. They were now right next to the Meat Department and it's door. The only bad thing about being in this location was the fact that the backroom where the stairs and elevators were at the other end of the back lobby.

Alan popped his head out the bakery doors and took a quick look around. He saw the swinging doors to the backroom, but there were several carts trolling just in front of them, while others traveled routinely up and down the aisles.

Besides the regular grocery carts, Alan also saw a motorized mobility cart and a kid's cart which was shaped like a race car. He used to think how awesome it would be if carts could move themselves and you would not need to push them. Now that he was witnessing it firsthand, he realized how creepy that was.

Alan held his index finger up to his lips to show Grace to be quiet. He looked out once again, stepped outside, but immediately slipped through the Meat Department door. He held the door open slightly for Grace to pass through. Once she peered out and saw that it was clear, she darted into the Meat Department and joined Alan.

CHAPTER 13

Mike's Meat

The meat department lights were completely off. The only light streamed in from the back-lobby filtering through multiple windows along the meat counter. There was a collection of knives on the tables lining the wall.

Grace looked at her bread knife and then at the knives on the tables. She noticed a large butcher's cleaver, picked it up, and tossed the bread knife to the side.

"Grab a knife or two also," she said. "You'll need something to protect yourself. We don't know what we'll run into."

Alan looked at the cleaver she was holding and at the other knives around the room. "What the hell is a knife going to do? I am grabbing the gun when we get the flashlights from Mr. Helovich's office. We'll grab the gun and then head down to meet your dragon pet and his devilish friend, Samael. Does your dragon have a name?"

"This isn't a joke."

"I know but give me a break. I'm freaking out here a little. Personally, I think I'm dealing with it quite well."

A knife flew by Alan's head and buried itself into the wall behind him.

"I think you need a knife," said Mike, who stood at the other end of the Meat Department, holding another, but larger knife.

"Mike? Mike, it's us. Alan. Grace. Come on man, we're not possessed," pleaded Alan.

"I know. Apparently, Samael thinks there's a virgin among you whose blood we need to break open the Gate. So, let's go down and visit him, shall we?"

"Virgin?" questioned Grace and then looked at Alan.

"Virgin?" questioned Alan and stared back at Grace.

"Oh, not me," they both responded in unison.

Another knife ripped through the air and lodged itself in the wall between them.

"Just to let you know, I'm not missing my target by accident. I'm warning you. The next one will be in one of your chests."

Alan looked at Mike, then at Grace and back to Mike. Panic filled his body and he got a little lightheaded. He looked down and saw the assortment of knives spread out on the table in front of him. Instinctively, he started picking up the knives and throwing them at Mike. He did not even attempt to look at his target and aim, he just focused on picking them up and throwing them as fast as he could in Mike's direction. When he ran out of knives, he paused for a moment, expecting a knife to come flying back at him and into his chest, but nothing happened.

He looked up and saw that most of the knives hit Mike directly in his chest, a couple in his head, and some in his stomach area. Mike had a surprised expression on his face as he looked down and saw the knives protruding from his body. His body twitched twice and then he fell facedown onto the floor.

Grace and Alan stood there staring at him for a couple moments. Mike did not move.

"How d'you do that?" asked Grace.

"I don't know. I... I didn't even aim."

"Let's go through the meat locker to get to the back room. The door opens near the bathrooms and the stairs leading to the manager's office. We won't have to go onto the main floor then."

"Sounds good to me."

They opened the meat locker door and Alan took one more look back at Mike who lay motionless on the floor.

"Can the Lemures make him pop back up?"

"Only if he was possessed by them. If he were, he'd still be standing."

"What? You mean he's working for Samael of his own free will? That asshole!" He picked up another knife next to the meat locker and threw it at Mike. It completely missed him, hit the wall, and then bounced back towards Alan. Alan shut the door before the knife could hit him.

There were no sides of beef hanging to cure, just boxes of pre-cut meat pieces. Like the bakery, the Meat Department no longer employed their craft at the store level. Everything arrived pre-cut or pre-packaged. The illusion of what butchers had once crafted was lost to the modern way of streamlining and the mass production of meat products. Alan grabbed one of the hooks from the track overhead. Nothing moved. Everything was dead, like Grace had said. The monsters wanted nothing to do with dead animal parts.

In the backroom, the metal door from the meat locker opened. Grace and Alan stepped out. Grace held her cleaver out in front of her; ready to strike anything that moved. Alan held his meat hook, cautiously looking around the backroom for anything unusual. It appeared normal, almost too normal, which scared him. Streaks of blood made a wet trail from each of the swinging doors that came in from the main store area and lead to the produce elevator; some blood trailed down the stairwell to the basement.

As they passed the men's bathroom, they heard the hand dryer start, then it stop, there was some pounding on a metal surface and then the dryer started up again. Both Grace and Alan stopped in their tracks. Should they run for it? Should they just stay frozen? They looked at each other, unsure of what to do. Then, the door flew open and Paul walked out, waving his arms to clear the air. "Whew! I thought I was going to die in there! You don't want to go in there. Too many protein shakes."

Both Alan and Grace spun around at Paul with their weapons poised to attack.

"Alan? What's going on? Who's the hot little Asian girl?"

"I'm Dutch!" instinctively responded Grace.

"Oh, you must be a relative of Grace. She always says that."

"Yeah, something like that," responded Alan.

"What's with the meat hook and huge knife?"

Grace and Alan both looked at their weapons as they forgot they were holding them in position to strike Paul.

"Defending ourselves from the Lemures. They..." responded Grace.

Alan cut her off, "They're a gang. These Lemures robbed us. They locked us in the store. We're headed up to the Boss's office to call the police."

"What?" Grace looked at Alan confused.

Alan bent over and whispered to Grace. "Like he could even understand the truth?"

"Is Mandy okay? I was stuck on the can the whole time. She needs to clock out."

"You don't need to worry about her right now," replied Alan. "She lost her head at first, but we took care of it."

They walked over to the base of the stairs and looked up. Paul followed behind them, curious why they did not just run up to the office. "Are they still in the store?"

"Who?" asked Grace.

"The Monkey gang, Lemurs," responded Paul.

"Oh, hmm, not sure. Best to be careful." Alan stood at the base of the stairs and looked back at his roommate. Poor dude, he thought. Paul could never understand anything that Alan had seen so far this evening. It was probably better to be a dumb jock in this situation. No fear of something you cannot comprehend.

Alan looked up at the top of the stairs. Both the break room door and Mr. Helovich's door were closed. The entire backroom continued to be deathly quiet.

"You know if the door is shut, then it's locked. Mr. Helovich never leaves the door unlocked. Any thoughts on how you're going to open it? You don't have your keys, remember?" said Grace.

"Shit, that's right. I forgot. I'll just kick it down like I did the Booth door."

Paul laughed immediately to Alan's statement. "You? Kick down a door? Really? Let me do it. I have way more muscle and weight than both of you. Let me do it for you, buddy. Besides, I don't mind showing off my muscles to the little lady." He smiled at Grace and winked. He did not wait for their response and ran up the stairs.

Grace and Alan cautiously followed behind Paul as he ascended the stairs.

At the top, Paul aligned himself and then rushed the door like he was playing football, putting his entire shoulder into the door. The door creaked and shifted a bit but did not open. Again, he positioned himself and threw his entire body into it, but this time he busted the door open. The momentum was so great that when the door opened, Paul's entire body stumbled into the office.

The lights in the office turned on and Paul returned to the doorway. "See, nothing to it," he boasted.

Instantly, a gorilla-sized spider, with the deformed head of Mr. Helovich, grabbed Paul from behind and bit him on the shoulder and neck. As Paul struggled and stepped back, he bumped the door and it closed shut. Alan and Grace jumped and ran back down the stairs. They heard Paul's screams mixed with the noise of a thunderous scuffle coming from the office. The door shook several times, then someone or thing hit against it.

The noise ceased. Paul's screams faded.

"What the hell was that?" Alan exclaimed.

"Ssh. Keep it down. The Lemures are still around and might hear us."

Alan started pacing back and forth at the base of the stairs. "I'm not going up there! Did you see the size of that thing!"

"We need to get the flashlights. We can't go down there without light. Or a gun?"

Alan looked at the basement stairs next to the elevator and only saw darkness. He looked back up at the manager's office and then back at the basement stairs.

"Alan?"

"I'm thinking here. Give me a second. This isn't something I have an immediate answer for. Fuck, that was an enormous spider."

"Really," asked Grace. "Think about it?"

"It's a fucking spider with Mr. Helovich's head on it! Yes, I need to think about it."

Grace looked around for a moment, then walked over to the fire extinguisher on the wall and grabbed it. She headed back up the stairs to the office.

Alan followed her, looking a bit confused as to what she was going to do next. "What do you think you're doing with that?"

"Isn't it obvious?" asked Grace. "You're not the only one who watches horror movies. Don't they always use a fire extinguisher on insects? It freezes them or something like that?"

"Yes, but this bug is huge." He tried the doorknob to the break room, but it was locked. Damn, he thought. We could have rushed in there if we needed an escape from the office. Guess we'll just have to run back down the stairs.

Grace paused for a second when she reached the top step and looked at Alan. She then stepped forward and easily kicked in the broken door, rushing in while spraying the extinguisher all over the office.

She stopped spraying after a moment and looked around. She saw neither the spider nor Paul. The security monitors gave the only light to illuminate the room.

"It's safe to come in, Alan. Nothing's here."

He popped his head around the corner and looked in. She was correct. There was nobody or anything in the office. "Where'd they go? There aren't any windows open and no other door."

"I don't know," replied Grace as she searched the cabinets for some flashlights, which she found after opening a couple of drawers.

Alan watched the security monitors and could see the carts as they continued roaming around the main store's floor. The parking lot showed a bunch of carts still piled up against the store's exterior doors.

"Where's the gun kept?" asked Grace.

Alan continued to watch the monitors and noticed that the basement camera revealed that most of the basement lights were flickering just like those on the main store floor. Occasionally, he got a good image of the area. He then saw Missy walking around carrying a large bag over her shoulders in the basement.

"Harry?" mumbled Alan.

"Harry?"

"I meant Missy. She's down in the basement. It's a long story. Why's she down there?"

"Focus. The gun? Where does Mr. Helovich keep it?" Grace asked, irritated by Alan's lack of focus on the current situation.

Alan walked over to the desk and pulled out the handgun from the underside of the desktop where it had been Duct taped.

"Why would he tell you where he kept his gun?"

"He didn't. I saw him put it there once when I was still a Bagger years ago. He always keeps it loaded too." Alan checked and confirmed there were bullets in the gun.

"I know where the spider went." She walked passed Alan to the coat hooks on the wall. She looked down at the ground and there was a blood trail along the floor that stopped at the wall. She examined the hooks and then turned one. Part of the wall opened, revealing a hidden door.

"A secret door," Alan said in surprise. He had been up in this office many of times and never suspected this from Mr. Helovich. He was paranoid, yes, but Alan never guessed that his boss actually would have a secret passageway.

Grace pushed the door open as far as she could and then clicked on a flashlight. "Paul was dragged down this way." She tossed the other flashlight to Alan. "Let's go. I think this will be a better way to get into the basement."

"What are we waiting for? Let's go spider hunting. Does your dragon friend like spiders? Maybe he'll eat it before we find it?"

"Glad to see you're accepting all this so well."

CHAPTER 14

The Basement

Grace, then Alan, stepped out from the secret passage, which placed them behind the large cardboard baler. It was the same location where Mr. Helovich had emerged and witnessed the death of Luigi. It was also where the boss had been bitten by the possessed tarantula as he attempted to sneak away.

Cautiously, they crept out from behind the baler and scanned the area for any movement.

"Where do you think it went?" asked Alan. He hoped they would see it go in one direction and they would go in the opposite direction, but he had little confidence that his wish would come true.

"I don't know. The blood stops here in front of the baler."

Both of them quickly examined the various aisles of pallets visually, but saw nothing.

Silently, the spider's legs popped out of the baler as it slowly crawled out.

Alan looked at the puddle of blood where the trail stopped. He then noticed a couple of drops of blood hit the floor. Looking directly above where they stood, he saw Paul's body stuck to the ceiling by spider webs. Paul's head was partially severed and dangled, by a couple of tendons that kept the head attached to his body. Paul's eyes followed Alan as his body cautiously rotated.

"Look up!" whispered Alan.

As Grace looked up, Paul's head disconnected and fell to the floor splashing blood onto them.

His body remained securely fixed on the ceiling. His eyes looked back at her for a moment and then at Alan. The spider then grabbed Grace and attempted to pull her into the baler.

Alan stepped back away from the baler and pointed the gun at the mutated spider, but the beast strategically kept Grace between it and the barrel of the gun. "Grace, move. I'll hit you."

"What do you think I'm trying to do," she screamed as she struggled to break free from the spider's grip. She swung the cleaver at the spider and hit one of its legs. It loosened its hold on her and she dropped to the floor then rolled away. "Shoot it, dammit, shoot it!"

Alan pulled the trigger several times as the spider retreated inside the baler.

Grace stood up next to the control panel and hit the start button. The door dropped and closed, trapping the spider within it. The compactor compressed and crushed the monstrous spider. A high-pitched squeal emanated from the baler, as the spider's guts oozed out.

"Two for two. We're pros at this now," boasted Alan.

"4 for 4 actually. Ms. Pepper, Bob the Baker, Mike, and now Mr. Spider-Boss. Or, is it Mr. Boss-spider? But who's counting." Grace confidently snapped her head and flicked her hair off her shoulder. "Ready for our next fight."

"So, where to now, Dragon Lady?" asked Alan.

"What?"

"No. I meant, well, some of the other employees called you Dragon Lady behind your back. I just thought one of them knew something about you or saw your dragons in your apartment."

"I told no one nor had anyone visit my apartment before you. They probably called me that because of my age and catch me staring at you when you weren't looking. Don't get freaked out from that statement, please? Remember, I've always been young at heart, though my body wasn't. My life stopped right around your age."

Alan saw a slight grin on Grace's face. He thought for a moment about what she had just revealed to him. "You mean you like me in like 'like me'? Like REALLY like me?"

"It is, well, I am complicated as you know by now. I guess they thought I was a cougar since I was older than you."

"Really older than me, like a dragon. That's kind of funny if you stop and think about it. Kind of ironic."

"Glad you can find some humor in all of this. Let's move on."

They walked towards the produce area. The motorized pallet mover was still sticking halfway into the produce cold box. A trail of blood came out of the cold box and continued to the back of the basement.

"Luigi, no. They got him too."

"That blood trail continues to the back of the basement. That's where we'll find our entrance to the Temple. It was buried shortly after the earthquake, after the fight ended and Samael was locked up again. Then the Dragon Spirit covered it up to hide it from the world. But it looks like Mike rediscovered it."

The motorized pallet mover pulled out of the cold box and knocked Alan to the ground. Grace leaped onto the produce sink to avoid getting smashed by it.

"You okay?" asked Alan. He looked up and saw Grace unscathed, sitting in the sink.

The pallet mover switched its direction and headed towards Alan. He stood up and hopped onto the pallet next to him and climbed up the diaper boxes.

As soon as Alan was off the ground, the pallet mover changed directions again and backed up at full speed into the produce sink. Grace jumped out of the sink just in time to dodge the impact. She sprinted over to the nearest pallet and scaled a stack of unopened banana boxes.

As they looked down, the motorized pallet mover was searching for them as other possessed equipment rolled into the area. Like the grocery carts on the main floor, down here there were hand dollies, rolling racks, and hand-jacks that appeared out of nowhere and cruised up and down the pallet aisles.

"Lie low, they're dumb. They might not realize we're even up here," commented Grace as she waved her hands at Alan to get his attention.

"What? Really."

She motioned to him to lie flat on top of the stacked boxes.

The possessed equipment meandered around, randomly bumping into various pallets full of product, apparently not sure where Alan and Grace were hiding.

The Lemures were extremely stupid as they did not realize that the objects they were attempting to possess might or might not have something they needed, something like eyes to see or ears to hear. They couldn't communicate with each other either.

In these situations, the evil globs of goo had to rely on another being, like Samael, to direct them. Samael though had difficulty visualizing Grace in his head, as she was connected to the Dragon and Alan was blocked as well by being so close to Grace. So, Samael was unable to guide the Lemures towards them. Eventually, the Lemures just wandered away in different directions in search of human blood somewhere else.

Grace and Alan crawled along the tops of the various pallets towards the back of the basement. They reached the last row of pallets stacked near the chain-linked fence. The chain-link gate, a few feet away, was wide open. Between themselves and the gate were various carts, a wheelchair, and a couple of grocery dollies. None of them moved and did not appear to be possessed. The trail of blood went along the floor and past the gate, disappearing into a large hole, in the back wall of the basement. The hole itself was pitch black.

Grace and Alan, on top of two different pallets, were separated by an aisle between them. Both slid down the boxes as quietly as possible. Once they touched the ground, the carts, wheelchair, and dollies began moving towards them.

Alan immediately ran to Grace, grabbed her by the hand and pulled her along. "Run, jump!" He yelled out commands as they attempted to avoid all the possessed equipment. He held her hand as tight as possible, dragging her along with him. As they passed through the gate, he flung her forward as he twisted back around, grabbing the gate and slamming it shut. Alan then wedged himself against the gate as the carts and dollies rammed into it. He opened it for a brief second to grab the lock and chain to bring it inside with them. Alan then secured the chain, holding the gate shut and locked in place.

"Great, so how are we supposed to get out of here? That's probably our only escape route," complained Grace as she pulled herself out of the stack of cigarette boxes Alan pushed her into.

"I thought this was a one-way trip? We'll deal with it if we even make it back this way."

They pushed aside the cigarette cases to get to the dark opening in the wall. Alan with his flashlight and gun in hand, and Grace with her butcher cleaver and flashlight in hand, approached the hole like the skilled Ninjas they were not.

"Ladies first," said Alan as he stepped to the side and waved at her to proceed.

"Really?" questioned Grace. "Now you're going to pull the gentleman crap on me."

"It's your dragon friend and his devil buddy. I think you probably have a better understanding of what we'll be walking into than me."

"Fine," snapped Grace as she nudged him when she passed him by and approached the hole. He was correct.

She was the only one who had experienced this before and knew what they were walking into. She figured if he truly knew what they were going to face, he might abandon her as soon as she told him all the details. Her fear was he would leave, and she would have to face it alone.

She prayed the Dragon Spirit could hold on a little longer and keep the Gate closed until they reached it. If Samael freed himself before they got there, she knew it would be almost impossible to force him back through it.

Last time he was too powerful to be killed and the Green Dragon only defeated him by using a surprise maneuver. The Green Dragon prevented Samael from launching a full head on assault by leaping to the side and avoiding Samael's charge. Samael lost his balance and rolled onto the ground, back through the Gate. The Dragon Spirit immediately separated from its bond with Grace's soul and shut the Gate, sealing it again with its life force. It may not have been strong enough to kill

Samael with brute force but it had opted to use something unexpected. It worked, Samael did not expect it, and all were supposedly safe.

"Wait!" said Alan, as he grabbed her shoulder and stopped her from stepping through the hole.

That startled her for a second and she ended up taking a couple steps away from him. She gazed at the hole again. "What? What is it?" She was concerned that maybe he saw something she had not. Perhaps a trap or something.

He bent down and opened a box and pulled out a large bottle of whiskey. He smiled at her as he opened it and took a large gulp, coughing immediately with the first swallow. "Want some?"

"No thanks," she responded, disgusted by the thought of it.

"My dad told me whiskey was the best way to numb the pain and I almost never, no, actually I've never agreed with him, but in this case, I believe he was right."

"Pain? Are you hurt? I don't see any wounds."

"Not yet. I have a feeling once we enter there, we're going to be in a whole hell of pain. I'm just prepping for it. I always like to be prepared." He offered the bottle to her again.

She looked at the bottle, then at him, and then back at the bottle. She grabbed it without a word and downed a large gulp and also started coughing immediately. "We need to keep moving. If Samael breaks through the Gate and there is no human soul for the Dragon Spirit to bond with and take solid form, then Samael can easily destroy it. At that point, there'll be no way to stop him."

"Lead on fearless leader!" he smiled and winked at her then took another chug of whiskey.

Grace disappeared into the darkness in the wall and Alan followed right behind her. As they traveled along the tunnel, they followed the blood trail. Articles of clothing and shoes were scattered along the way. They actually saw grocery aprons with name tags still attached. Alan noticed a piece of flowery torn fabric from the sundress that the customer in the wheelchair was wearing when he had encountered her earlier in the day.

The abandoned train tunnel was dimly lit by a couple of lanterns resting on the tables. Digging tools were scattered about. The opening to the path that led up to the Temple area was no longer illuminated by a green glow, but now flickered with yellow light from torches that burned along the path's walls.

On the other side of the tunnel, where the passage led back to the store, flashes of light came from Grace's flashlight as she and Alan stumbled out of the narrow passage. Grace shined her flashlight around to examine the new area. Alan followed her and used his light to help expand the view of their surroundings in the tunnel.

"Looks like a train tunnel. But it's caved in on either end," commented Alan.

"Interesting. So, Mike found the haunted train tunnel. City engineers collapsed it shortly after the opening of the Twin Peaks Tunnel Line in 1917. They built two tunnels originally. They did not know they had built this one so close to the Gate. Horrible things happened on the first day they started running trains through it."

Both continued to examine the tunnel. Alan put the gun down on the table as he rummaged through the various tools and items on the tables. "What kinds of horrible things?"

"The first train that passed through this area, arrived at the next station with all of its passengers slaughtered to death. No one survived the trip. They figured the person who killed everyone had committed suicide just before the train arrived at the station. The same thing happened with the second train, except this time one person survived the carnage. It was a five-year-old girl. Somehow when the rescuers were digging, they unknowingly freed several Lemures. The city immediately collapsed the tunnel and blamed it on some gases that made the passengers go insane."

Missy appeared from the darkness behind Alan and grabbed the gun on the table without him noticing.

"Looks like we'll get to add two more bodies to this haunted tunnel," taunted Missy as she flashed the gun at them. She placed a large bag on the table which opened slightly revealing a large amount of cash. "You, get over here next to your boyfriend." She motioned with her gun towards Grace. Grace tried not to trip over anything as she moved next to Alan, stepping over some tools on the ground. "Wow, you moved on quickly, I see. So, she's your rebound from me," Missy said, not as a question but as a statement. It was not out of jealousy, but a total non-emotional, sarcastic comment meant to smash Alan's ego that Missy couldn't pass up.

"Harry, I mean Missy, are you crazy? What are you doing? And why in the hell did you steal my keys?"

"Don't you ever call me Harry! So, you finally figured that out? Guess you aren't as stupid as I thought you were."

"You and Mike needed to get into the cigarette and liquor stock area," replied Grace.

"Impressive, China Doll is smarter than you, Alan," said Missy.

"She's Dutch," responded Alan immediately without a second thought.

Grace smiled internally in admiration of Alan for defending her.

"What, one of Grace's granddaughters? Should have figured. Doesn't matter, anyway. You will both be dead in a few moments."

Alan stepped towards Missy. "You will not hurt us. I don't believe you will shoot me or her. You might hate me, but not enough to kill me. I don't think so."

Missy quickly raised the gun aimed at Alan's head and pulled back the hammer. "Step back."

Alan stopped immediately.

She lowered the gun and shot next to his foot. "The next one is between your legs. Want to test your luck?"

Alan stepped back towards Grace again while covering his groin.

"We had it all planned out. In and out in a couple of weeks. Get into the U.S. Mint vault, rob the store, then disappear. But then Mr. Helovich promoted you and gave you the keys to the store. Not to Mike, as the new night crew manager, oh no. So, we had to improvise and get them from you.

"We? You and Mike are partners?" asked Alan in disbelief.

"Engaged. Partners in crime and in love. Sorry, Alan, but someone else has always had my heart."

"Mike?" responded Alan puzzled.

"Mike!" responded Grace as she saw the outline of a figure approach Missy from behind. As the figure entered the light, Grace could see that it was a bloody Mike. The knives still protruded from his head and body like the last time Grace and Alan had left him lying on the floor in the Meat Department.

"Yes, Mike," whispered Mike into Missy's ear.

She smiled hearing his familiar voice and relaxed her stance with the gun.

"And you're right my love, I have your heart," whispered Mike as his arm burst through her chest clutching her still beating heart.

Missy saw the hand sticking out of her chest with her heart beating. The gun went off and knocked over the table that the lanterns were on, causing the room to darken. Missy's body went limp and fell back into Mike.

Alan and Grace disappeared into the darkness. They had turned off their flashlights as soon as the gun took out the lanterns and retreated towards the back of the tunnel near one of the collapsed ends. They hid behind some wreckage.

Alan and Grace watched in silence as Mike carried Missy's body to the large opening at the far side of the tunnel wall and headed towards the Temple.

CHAPTER 15

THE TEMPLE

Mike struggled a bit as he dragged Missy's body towards the pond and the Sacrifice Tree. Not for his lack of strength, but lack of coordination because the Lemures had found him dying on the floor in the Meat Department and re-entered his body, so he could continue to be of service to Samael.

The Lemures were also the ones who ripped out Missy's heart. Mike, himself, would never have done that. He loved her. He did not want to do it, but they made him, or his body, do it. It was tearing him emotionally apart, trapped inside his mind, replaying what had just happened. He had so easily killed her. She was the one that he loved so much that he had sold his soul to Samael, in the hot desert, to be able to return to her and marry her. Now, all his sacrifices were for nothing. He just killed her and was now placing her body on the Sacrifice Tree so that Samael could free himself. Mike was furious.

All the torment he had endured through this ordeal was not worth the cost. He should have died out there in the desert. Missy would still be alive. All this now made him realize he no longer had a reason to live anymore. But the Lemures continued to control his body and there was nothing he could do about it, no matter how hard he tried to fight back. He could not control his body. His thoughts were the only thing he could still control.

He watched helplessly as his body continued working by itself. He thought about all the people that they dragged down here. How horrible it must have been for each of them seeing what was going on, feeling everything, but unable to do anything to stop it.

He watched as his body picked her up and tossed her on the Sacrifice Tree. Her blood drained out of her body, then it shriveled up and turned to ashes almost immediately. Her blood flowed out and up the groove in the floor towards the Gate. The emerald light surrounding the portal of the open Gate flickered and dimmed, then went out completely.

Samael approached the Gate, scrutinized it as the light faded. "Sacrificing your own love, just to free me? What an honorable gesture."

Mike wanted to curse Samael. He wanted to rush at him and take the knives from his body and drive them deep into Samael's forehead.

Suddenly, it dawned on Mike that Samael did not need virgin blood, but blood from someone Mike loved. That was it. He had to sacrifice his own love to break the Dragon's seal over the gate, and Mike was foolish enough to fall for it. This enraged Mike beyond any sanity he had left; a shell of man remained.

The Dragon Spirit energy faded completely as Samael was talking, but as he finished speaking the illuminating emerald light re-appeared across the portal, within inches of Samael.

"I would have thought that type of love-bond would have blown the Dragon Spirit completely away. But obviously it was more lust than genuine love between the two of you."

"Fuck you!" thought Mike, but then realized he had said it out loud. Wow. How was he able to say that, even with the Lemures controlling him? It surprised him, but he realized that the Lemures were probably releasing their control to leave him, as Samael would probably sacrifice him next. "I'm sorry, Samael. There's been so many bodies and so much blood. I just want my freedom. I, I thought this would have worked."

"You want your freedom? Do you know how many years I've been waiting for my freedom? Don't even attempt to tell me about your torment. If I shared mine with you, your mind would melt." Samael sniffed the air. "Hold on there." He continued to sniff the air. "You might be free sooner than you thought. Why don't you welcome our guests?" Samael waved his arm out and pointed towards Alan and Grace, who were sneaking up the steps and onto the Temple grounds.

Grace had her butcher's cleaver out, while Alan carried a mining pick he had picked up along the way.

"This would have been so much easier if you had just come down with me when I asked you in the Meat Department. Now, Missy is dead and you both will be dead soon as well." Mike's rage was blinding him, as he blamed the two of them for Missy's death. Had they just come down with him earlier. Had they not attempted to kill him, then these Lemures would not have had to enter his body to keep him alive. Missy would not be dead. He tried to shift the blame to anyone else, but himself.

Alan and Grace got closer to Mike, who stood next to the Gate where Samael stood, on the other side of the portal. The emerald shimmering energy was the only thing keeping Samael from entering their world.

"That must be Samael, nice bald head and horns look," commented Alan.

"Yep, and he has his friendly face on but don't let that fool you," remarked Grace.

"With horns in his forehead, I don't think I'll forget who's the devil around here," remarked Alan. He was not trying to be a smartass or joke around, but he was out of his comfort zone by a longshot and didn't know how else to handle the situation.

"Mike, why are you helping him? Do you know what will happen if he enters our world?" asked Grace.

"He mended my body and gave me back my life and only asked for a small favor. I don't care what he does once he's freed."

"Welcome back, Grace. It's been a while, at least in your human years," snarled Samael as they approached. "How's dear old Dad? Oh, yes, still dead?"

Grace's face glared with anger, the cleaver raised above her head. She quickly gained control of herself and lowered the cleaver.

Mike stared at Grace. "Grace? That's you?"

Samael continued talking to Grace and ignored Mike. "You don't look like you've aged a bit. Funny how the bonding of a human soul to a Dragon Spirit works. The residual affects do remarkable things to the human body. You know if you bond again, you will die this time. You weren't strong enough to kill me last time, so why do you think you can this time."

"Lies! All lies. That's all your kind do!" yelled Grace, but she revealed a slight reservation in her tone.

"Am I lying? Then why hasn't the Spirit bonded with you yet? It must know your soul will not give it the strength it needs to defeat me."

Samael turned to Mike. "Mike, grab her and hang her on the Tree of Sacrifice. The last thing she'll see before dying will be the barrier dissolving to nothing. It will be her own blood that kills the Dragon Spirit."

Mike's body responded to Samael's commands instantly, even though Mike's mind was still trying to understand everything that was happening around him. Mike approached Grace to grab her, but Alan stepped in and swung the pick at him and buried it deep into the side of his head. Mike's body did not seem phased by the impact of the spike. His mind felt the pain and internally he screamed out. He wished the nightmare would be over.

It surprised Alan to see that Mike did not drop to the ground when the pick struck and then stuck in his head. Mike just reached up and pulled it out and smiled back at Alan.

"Would you like to go first," Mike said to Alan.

"Oh shit! Lemures, Grace. Lemures are in him. Run." Alan spun around to retreat but came face to face with a badly burned Baker Bob, the tips of his mustache still on fire. He even held his smoking, rolling pin high above his head. The blur of the rolling pin and the following darkness told Alan that he had just been clobbered by Baker Bob.

Grace swung her cleaver at Baker Bob as she screamed for Alan. But she knew immediately that he did not hear her, as she saw his limp body roll to the side. Grace focused all her rage into her swing with the cleaver at Baker Bob. She got a direct hit to his neck and popped his head off. The body dropped to the ground. Then she kicked the head into the Gate. Baker Bob's head disintegrated as it reached the barrier and touched the Dragon's Spirit protecting the Gate.

She was so focused on turning her attention back to Alan to see if he was okay that she forgot about Mike, who kicked the cleaver from her hand and then slugged her across the jaw, knocking her out cold.

Mike picked up Grace's limp body and carried it towards the Tree of Sacrifice.

"Perfect! I will enjoy watching this bitch shrivel up into dust," squealed Samael as the joy of the vision of Grace disintegrating in a few seconds was overwhelming him.

The emerald barrier flickered several times across the Gate. Samael studied it for a moment, then he raised his hands while forming a large fireball over his head. He shot it directly into the barrier and the force blew both Samael and Mike, who was already struggling to carry Grace, away from the Gate.

From the darkness Samael's laughter echoed, then he reemerged, approaching the Gate. "Well, Michael, it looks like your little girlfriend's blood did the job. We just needed to give it a little time to work." Samael walked through the portal and into the Temple. The emerald barrier no longer existed.

Mike's mind grieved hearing those words about his girlfriend. Though they may have made bad choices in life, and according to Samael they had sinned so much that God would never forgive them, he knew Missy loved him. That genuine love was probably the only innocence she had left in her. That thought, itself, crushed his heart, his soul, if he still had one. His desire and drive to free Samael died. His very will to live evaporated. Yet, his body continued on, controlled by the Lemures.

Even though it was the Lemures that ripped her heart out, the reality was that it was he who had really killed her by accepting Samael's offer. His selfish wish to stay alive at all costs was the biggest sin, which led to her death. It was his decisions that led to this moment. He was so tied up with his thoughts that he did not even notice the Samael was standing next to him in the room, no longer on the other side of the Gate.

"We'll still put her on the Sacrifice Tree, so we can torture her slowly and drain out her life. Gradually though, so she does not pass out and can watch her own destruction 'til the very end."

Samael waved his left hand and Grace's body lifted off Mike's shoulder and flew into the branches of the Sacrifice Tree.

The thorns lengthened as they entered her body. She awoke screaming and unable to break free from the tree. Her entire body trembled and then her hair whitened while her smooth skin wrinkled.

Alan stood up and rushed to Grace's side. He grabbed the belt around her waist and tried to pull her off. Tears ran down her face as she continued to scream in pain. She looked back at him and could only shake her head NO, as the pain increased, causing her to scream out again.

The thorns continued to grow, now long enough to pass through her belt and into Alan's hand as he still tried to pull her from the tree. He now screamed as he realized the thorns had penetrated his hand.

Suddenly, something invisible wrapped itself around Alan's neck and pulled him away from Grace, along the ground, to where Samael and Mike stood.

"Hello, Alan. I have not properly introduced myself. Yet, we met in a dream once. I'm Samael, your Lord and Master."

"Go to Hell!" responded Alan.

"Oh, I have, and well, I prefer to stay here for a while. Perhaps you would like to go there yourself? Hum?"

Samael looked back at the Gate and then at Alan. "Care to take a trip?" Samael flicked his hand towards the gate and Alan's body flew towards it, but then stopped in mid-flight. "Wait. Come back."

Alan's body floated back to Samael. All of this was controlled by Samael, even though Samael talked to Alan as if Alan, himself, had a choice in the matter.

"Michael, devoted servant, you have completed your end of the bargain. I'm feeling a bit generous at the moment."

"So, I'll get my life back?" begged Mike, though he was not sure what that would mean to him, now that the woman who meant everything to him was dead.

"Yes, and well, no."

"Lying to me again?"

Alan, though suspended in the air and unable to move his body, could still hear and even talk. He was surprised by the comment that came flying out of his mouth since he didn't think he'd be able to speak or move. "He's a devil. You expected him not to lie to you? What'd you expect from Samael after all was said and done, he'd be your BFF?"

Mike slugged Alan across the face and Alan spun in circles like a piñata, suspended before Samael and Mike.

"Your own body appears to be beyond my powers of repair. Technically, you're dead once the Lemures exit you. Even I can't fix it. But I could switch your soul to Alan's body, if you like?"

Mike stepped closer to Alan and inspected his body, like he was inspecting a new car he was thinking of buying. He even squeezed one of Alan's biceps. "He's pretty scrawny and not as good-looking as me."

"Being choosy now? He's younger than you and you could go back to the gym and put some muscle on those bones. As for the looks, well, I'm not God."

"Hey!" responded Alan. Alan's floating body dropped to the ground as he felt the invisible force around him release its grip.

Mike reached down and grabbed Alan to help him stand up. While trying to stand up, Alan swayed a little and bumped into Mike and then into

Samael to stablize himself. He felt immense heat from the slight contact he had made with Samael. Mike grabbed Alan's face and looked closely at him.

"Blue eyes, I've always wished I had blue eyes," Mike said. "I accept the offer."

"I'm sorry," replied Alan. "But I'm still using this body at the moment."

Samael chuckled. "You're just keeping it warm for Mike."

"I'll take a rain check on that." Alan threw his entire weight into pushing both of them away and sprinted towards Grace. He had almost made it to her, but again the invisible grip wrapped around his throat. He stopped in his tracks. He continued to reach out to Grace.

Grace was reaching out with all her strength to touch him as well. Tears continuing to run down her face.

Unexpectedly, tears ran down Alan's face as he reached out for Grace. His dream was coming true; so close yet unable to get any closer. Is this what that dream meant? Was it warning him of how his life would end?

Mike watched in astonishment at the determination of both trying to touch each other, even though they were at the very edge of their own deaths. Did they think by some miracle that would free them? Or perhaps some fairytale magic would save them just with a touch? An overpowering wave of emotions hit Mike as he realized their driving force was that of their real love for each other. Both willing to sacrifice themselves for the other.

"When will you learn, you're only delaying the inevitable," snorted Samael.

"As soon as you learn to check your pockets," squeaked Alan, forcing a grin of satisfaction as he endured the choking grip around his throat.

What? Mike thought to himself. What was Alan talking about? This guy's tenacity amazed Mike as he seemed to never give up and continued to fight for survival. Mike knew a lot of soldiers that would have given up the fight a long time ago.

Both Mike and Samael looked down and saw a stick of dynamite tucked into their pockets. The wick was already lit and disappeared into the stick. They looked back at Alan just as the dynamite exploded.

The blast threw Alan back and he landed next to the pond. He hit his head on the edge. His vision blurred as he watched Grace's body shrivel up as all her blood drained. He passed out and traveled into a dark place where he felt nothing, no pain, and no worries; just floating through emptiness.

CHAPTER 16

Samael's Dance

When Alan awoke, he noticed the torches still illuminating the Temple. There was no apparent movement in the area. The Gate was closed now. No energy barrier covered it. He saw the charred remains of Mike's clothes, which had blown several feet away from where he had been standing before the blast. A column had collapsed and covered Samael's body. One of his hooves stuck out but did not move.

Alan wobbled to stand up and then rushed to the Sacrifice Tree but the only thing that remained of Grace was a piece of her skin with the Green Dragon tattoo; everything else was gone.

The tree could not dissolve that piece of her body. It had dried up again, along with the pond, and no sign of her blood.

"Grace. You stubborn old girl. You had a choice!" He reached up and gently lifted the piece of skin off the tree. He kissed it lightly and then carefully rolled it up. "At least I can bury this part you." He stumbled along the path back towards the abandon tunnel.

The rubble covering Samael vibrated and then shook. Samael's body expanded. As it grew, the debris from the column rolled off and away from him.

Alan looked back and struggled to pick up his pace. He had to leave the area quickly as he clearly saw Samael's body growing.

The rocks flew away in all directions as Samael, now twice as large as he was before, sprang to his feet, snarling madly. He now radiated flames all around him and his head was no longer human but that of a large bull, with long horns and burning red eyes.

Trying to find some type of humor in this situation, all Alan could think was that this must be Samael's mean face which Grace had warned him about. He did not like it either. "Crap!" exclaimed Alan as he used every effort to reach the abandoned train tunnel.

Samael heard Alan's remark and charged him full force, head down, and horns pointed directly at Alan's heart. Samael hit the wall and entrance to the abandoned tunnel with such force that Alan was hurled further inside it. By this time, Samael's size was not to his advantage since he had grown too large to fit through the opening.

Alan picked himself up off the ground from inside the tunnel. Luckily, he had landed next to, and not on top of, the pile of digging tools which very possibly could have impaled him.

The tunnel shook as the crashing sounds of Samael's head, ramming against the passageway leading into the abandoned tunnel, echoed. With each hit, pieces broke away and widened the entrance. On the fourth impact, debris fell everywhere, and Samael burst his way into the tunnel.

His flaming body illuminated the entire passage, leaving no place for Alan to hide. Samael scanned the area closely, looking for Alan, finally locating him hiding behind an over-turned table. Samael roared wildly and charged him.

The table, along with Alan, flew into the air. Along the way, Grace's tattooed skin slipped from Alan's hand and glided off in another direction. Alan and the table landed at the far end of the collapsed tunnel among tons of debris. Furiously satisfied, Samael approached Alan, confident that in the next moments he would rip this little human into tiny pieces. Samael kicked away any debris that stood in his way as he approached his target.

"Oh, come on Alan, you can't be dead yet. Let's play a little more."

A strange emerald light appeared and its intensity grew from behind Samael. Since his focus was solely on Alan, he had not notice it yet. Samael lifted the now twisted table and expected to see the Alan cowering, begging for his life. But Alan was not behind the table. At that point, the emerald light had intensified enough to overpower Samael's own flames which now reflected as flickers on the wall.

"NO! You should be dead!" screamed Samael as he whipped around and faced the Green Dragon. The emerald dragon faced Samael confidently. Its glowing emerald body solidified as its exterior skin fused shut. A glimpse of Grace's body was visible but disappeared, as the dragon completed its transformation into its full physical form.

The force of the Green Dragon's roar reverberated throwing Samael up against the wall of the tunnel. Samael attempted to push back against it but was forced to the side, out of the direct blast of the voice. Once freed, he rolled to the dragon's side and jumped on its back. Samael stretched out his arms in an attempt to crush the dragon as he steadied himself.

The dragon wildly twisted and turned while it dashed around the tunnel, attempting to shake Samael off its back.

Alan had been only a few feet from the table when Samael lifted it. Had the emerald light not drawn Samael's attention, Alan would have been his snack.

Alan was curled into a fetal position on the heap of rubble only a few feet away. He watched in awe as these two gigantic creatures engaged in a fight to the death. That is, if either creature could actually die.

Alan saw Grace's body for just a moment, suspended inside the body of the shimmering emerald dragon just before it finished taking its solid form.

How is that possible since there was nothing left of her after the tree turned her into ashes? But why question it now, he thought, with everything else he had witnessed this evening.

"Doesn't look like she's strong enough for you to completely materialize," laughed Samael as he tightened his grip on the dragon. The Green Dragon momentarily took full physical form but then reverted temporarily to a translucent form, and then back to its solid body.

The dragon rolled one way, then the other, tossing and turning, but it could not break Samael's grip.

Alan had to help, but how? What could he do to have any effect on these massive creatures? He frantically searched the surrounding area but only found the same pieces of digging equipment he had seen before, nothing new. He paused for a moment to think of options, then realized he was right next to the entrance leading back to the Temple. Maybe there was something back at the Temple he could use? The Gate was closed, and too small now since Samael's size was larger than that Gate itself.

A horrible realization overtook Alan. A deep feeling of doom filled his being as he realized there was nothing he could do to stop Samael from escaping into the city, and the world, if the Green Dragon could not kill him now, before he reached the surface.

Alan suppressed his apocalyptic thoughts when his nostrils inhaled the stench of scorched flesh and his eyes caught the image of a person standing next to him.

Mike's charred remains now stood next to Alan and he wondered how in hell that was even possible but then reasoned that if this truly was hell, anything was possible. The Lemures just wouldn't let Mike die. Hadn't Mike seen Alan standing there already? If so, he would have attacked by now, right? Alan thought as he remained motionless.

Mike watched the struggle between Samael and the emerald dragon. He did not even notice Alan.

Alan's gaze returned to the epic struggle before them.

Samael had pinned the dragon down while it was in a partially translucent state. He fiercely plunged his claws into the dragon, attempting to reach Grace, who remained suspended within the middle of the dragon's body.

Alan instinctively shouted, "No!" he yelled. Shit, he thought, he just alerted Mike and now had to face him since he was still only a few feet away. Alan turned towards Mike, ready to defend himself, but was surprised that Mike's charred remains did not attack him.

Mike, with one eye hanging out of its socket and the other one still intact, stared at Alan. His crispy flesh continued to crackle as he attempted to point at the creatures, but more specifically, Grace. Mike then pointed to a long iron pike on the ground and moved his finger towards Samael, down towards one of his hooves. Mike repeated the motion several times for Alan to see.

Alan, ignoring any distracting thoughts that this was going to be a bad idea, even though he knew it was, scrambled over to the pike and picked it up. He looked back at Mike.

Mike continued to point at Samael's hooves.

Alan circled around to the back of Samael, away from his direct sight, and bent down closer to Samael's hooves. He glanced over at the dragon as it turned translucent again. He could see that Samael's claw had reached into the dragon far enough that it was inches from Grace. Alan sprinted and drove the pike directly above the back side of Samael's hoof and into his flesh.

Samael's reaction was even greater than Alan had hoped. Samael's scream rattled the entire chamber and then his hoof struck Alan directly in the chest, flinging him across the room. But this unintended event also enabled Samael to thrust his claw further into the dragon, allowing him to grab Grace and pull her out. The Dragon Spirit faded away as soon as Grace was removed.

Samael stood up, holding Grace in his claw. He attempted to take a step towards Alan who was now at the other end of the tunnel but stumbled as the pike drove deeper into his hoof. He looked down and saw the cause of his pain and easily removed it. Samael threw the pike at Alan. The weapon embedded itself into the wall a few inches above his head.

"Oh, I missed, or did I? Here, catch your beloved," Samael snarled, as he tossed Grace directly at the protruding end of the pike.

Alan stood up and attempted to shield Grace from landing on the end of the pike. Fortunately, he did block her from being impaled and cushioned her impact. Unfortunately, his shoulder was skewered by the pike. Alan found it difficult to move while holding Grace's unconscious body but tried his best while pinned to the wall.

Samael approached them. "Such pathetic little mortals, and yet you two have been the biggest pains in my ass. I'll pick you both apart, piece by piece, like little insects."

Alan wanted to protect Grace from Samael, though there was not much he could do while stuck to the wall. He struggled with every inch of his being to defend her. Alan then noticed behind Samael that Mike's charred remains were walking towards the center of the tunnel, though Mike was starring upwards and not at them. So, Mike was not interested in gloating over Samael killing them, thought Alan. What was more interesting in the tunnel than this?

Suddenly, Samael's immense body blocked Alan's view and he could no longer see Mike. He did not have time to question how he could have seen Mike in the distance with only the light from one lantern which was knocked onto the ground, at the other end of the tunnel, and the flames from Samael's body.

Mike stood in the middle of the chamber as a light intensified over him with the focus of a spotlight, from an unknown origin. He then dropped to his knees.

Samael, focused on his human toys, kneeled and lowered his head so that his large bull nostrils breathed directly into Alan's face. "I do like my humans on a skewer, how'd you know?"

Without warning, A supernatural, angelic, golden light radiated from the ceiling and down the walls filling the entire tunnel.

Samael noticed the walls turn to a golden radiance. He sprang up and turned around. On the ceiling of the tunnel was a long, snake-like golden dragon, materializing as it engulfed Mike's charred remains. Mike welcomed the peace and tranquility that the Golden Dragon Spirit offered him. Mike had prayed to God as he watched Alan attack Samael with the pike. He asked God to forgive him for his foolishness and cowardice to accept his own fate, and all the evils he had committed in his life. He then asked God to spare Grace and Alan from Samael's wrath. His prayer was answered as the Gold Dragon engulfed him and the two merged into one inseparable being.

"That's my soul!" screamed Samael. "We had a deal! He is mine!"

The glistening Gold Dragon dropped from the ceiling and wrapped its snake-like body completely around Samael, who struggled to break free. Unsuccessful, Samael then attempted to blow fire into the face of the dragon, which began to dissolve its outer skin layer by layer. He was able to free one of his arms. Samael took another deep breath in an attempt to spray more fire but the dragon's head regenerated rapidly as it turned to bite Samael's free arm, ripping it out of its socket. It tossed the arm into the air, opened its mouth, and swallowed it whole.

Samael, because of the intense pain, lost all sanity and attacked the dragon biting at the dragon's body. He immediately spit out chunks of dragon flesh, as his lips and mouth began to dissolve from the dragon's gold blood which was dripping from his mouth. The drops of golden blood dissolved pieces of Samael's body.

Samael struggled as he tried to walk back to the Temple and back to the Gate. The weight of the Gold Dragon, tightly wrapped around his body, slowed him down tremendously.

Samael approached the Gate. He tried to open it with his one remaining arm but it would not open. He then banged on it several times. Exhausted, he collapsed to his knees in front of the Gate.

The golden dragon slithered off him and turned to face him.

"I'm sorry, my friend, but you will not seal this Gate! We have plans." Samael claimed as he gathered all his remaining energy into a fiery ball and shot it towards the dragon.

The Gold Dragon made no attempt to avoid the approaching energy blast, and opened its mouth swallowing it.

Samael responded by rushing the dragon with his horns, aimed directly at its head.

The dragon slid quickly to the side and up the wall. It struck back at Samael with lightning speed, encircling itself around him again. It raised its head high above Samael and then descended on him devouring his head, horns and all. Samael's headless body went limp and dropped to the ground. The dragon loosened its grip and slithered off Samael's body.

The dead body ignited into small flames and dissipated into ashes.

The dragon then slithered up the steps to the Gate and transformed into gold energy, spreading itself across the gate, permanently sealing it for all eternity. The glow continued to spread throughout the temple and into the train tunnel where Alan and Grace lay motionless. As the golden light passed over them, Alan regained his strength and was able to move again. His wounds were healed. The end of the pike, lodged in Alan's shoulder, dissolved away. Alan awoke and watched as the golden gleam continued to move over Grace's body. Grace's hair turned from white to black and her wrinkles faded away. Her body reverted to that of the young girl she had been when she had first encountered the Dragon Spirit years ago.

"Grace, we did it. We fucking did it!" Alan gently shook her to wake her up.

She did not respond but continued to lie motionless. He lifted her body to a sitting position and pulled down the collar of her shirt as he checked her shoulder and the back of her neck. There was no tattoo of a green dragon.

"Are you trying to take advantage of a girl while she's sleeping?" asked Grace as she moved her shirt back into place.

"I can't get anything past you," he said as he hugged her tightly. Alan watched as the gold light traveled down Grace's leg, healing whatever it touched. Alan noticed that Grace's torn pants mended themselves as the gold beam passed over them. "That's cool, the gold light is healing everything!"

"Gold Light?" asked Grace. She sat up and looked around, witnessing what Alan was watching. The light appeared to have a life of its own as it traveled throughout the tunnel.

"But who? Whose soul did the Dragon Spirit bond with? I don't understand?" asked Grace.

"I think it was Mike's," He responded thinking back and remembering seeing Mike in the middle of the tunnel, illuminated where there was no light source in the middle of the tunnel.

Grace observed the gold light engulfed the entire area wiping away any of the blood and evil presence. A couple of straggling Lemures fleeing towards the passage leading to the store were overtaken by the light and dissolved in mid-stride.

"We need to get out of here. The Gate is sealed. The Dragon Spirit will erase all evidence that this Hell Gate ever existed. We don't want to be a part of the erasing."

Alan helped Grace stand up. They ran through the small passage and headed back into the basement.

As they entered, the gold light had traveled a few feet ahead of them. The motorized pallet movers and dollies were still hitting against the chain gate but when the light passed over them, the equipment stopped moving and remained motionless. The chain-linked gate unlocked itself and opened.

"It's going after all the Lemures now," commented Grace.

"I like your dragon friend. Let's follow behind the light then. No reason to get ahead of it and have to fight off any monsters around here."

Alan and Grace walked up the stairs towards the main floor. They paced themselves to stay a few feet behind the golden light as it spread out along the stairwell and up through the two freight elevators. All traces of blood vanished.

As they reached the main floor of the store, Alan and Grace paused for a breath at the bottom of the stairs that lead up to the Manager's office and break room.

The break room door abruptly opened and Peli flew down the stairs and ran into them.

"Oh my god, what time is it? I fell asleep in the break room. Why are the lights so bright?" Peli asked shielding her eyes.

"You've been asleep in the break room all night?" asked Alan.

"Hmm, No. I was just on my break. Don't tell Mr. Helovich. I'm sorry. I'll clean up anything you want or get carts all day. Promise. How long have I been asleep?"

Grace looked carefully at Peli. "I think we found our virgin."

"I think you're right," chuckled Alan.

"Virgin? Me? What's it to you anyways?" she barked at Grace.

"It's a long story. She didn't mean anything bad about it. It's an honorable thing," replied Alan. "Hey, she can't be the virgin. What about Lily?"

"Lily? She's my little sister. I drop her off at daycare since it's on my way to work. Just because I have piercings and tattoos, that doesn't mean I'm anybody's baby-mama! My mother, Ms. Pepper, as you like to call her, was pregnant when she had her breakdown. I've been raising Lily myself."

Alan felt shame for being so hard on Peli earlier in the day. He was about to apologize for how he had treated her but then the entire building trembled as the light continued sweeping through the backroom area and out onto the shopping floor.

"Earthquake! Let's get out of here," yelled Alan while winking at Grace and smiled at Peli. They ran to the front of the store to exit. Alan did not see any traces of the horrible bloody trails or thorn-throwing artichokes in the front of the produce area as they passed the bins.

They approached the front door with the gold light continuing to sweep a few feet in front of them. They exited the store making it safely to the parking lot.

The fog had lifted, and the early morning darkness was brightened by the stars and moon above. On the horizon, the light of day was fast approaching. As Alan, Peli, and Grace ran out into the parking lot, they noticed grocery carts moving aimlessly about, bumping into everything or just traveling in circles.

The light was now a few feet behind them. A blast of energy engulfed the entire grocery store and some gold light radiated outwards to the scattered carts. The entire building rumbled and began to crumble away. All the grocery carts were being pulled back into the store. Some carts tried to roll away, but they could not break free from the glistening, golden light once it touched them. The carts were swallowed up into the collapsing building as it turned into a massive mound of rubble.

"Oh no! Nope! Don't expect me to clean this mess up. Nada. This is definitely not my job! I'm calling the Union if you think so. It's night crew's job for blowing up the store!" Peli pulled out her cell phone and dialed. She walked off mumbling into her phone screaming that she needed to be picked up and quitting her job.

Alan stood behind Grace and gently reached his arms around her and hugged her. He leaned down and whispered into her ear. "Let's go! We'll have just enough time to make it, I think."

"Make what? What are you talking about?" asked Grace. She felt his embrace and at first wanted to pull away, but realized she enjoyed it, so relaxed and fell back into him.

"Watch the sunrise over the bay from the Golden Gate Bridge."

"I can't!" was her immediate instinctive response, the same she had given for so many years. She chose to never be too far from the store.

"You're kidding, right? You've watched this damn Gate for over a hundred years. It doesn't exist anymore. You're free. Free. Let's be free together. The world is ours to explore. Together."

"Free? I... I would love to see the bridge. Then, get breakfast. Can we drive down the coast? I want to see the coast. I want to..."

"Slow down there. Let's get out of here before we miss the sunrise. We can discuss the rest over breakfast at the Cliff House."

"Lunch in Monterey? Watch the sunset at Morro Bay?" Grace's mind wildly raced with the overwhelming possibilities of where she could go. All these years, she had read about so many places she wanted to visit, and now she could.

"Whoa. Slow down." He said as he gently embraced Grace to contain her excitement. "Let's take our time. Sounds like there are a lot of things you want to do."

Grace looked down at the ground and after a couple of deep breaths looked back up at Alan. Her eyes were warm. A knowing smile grew while her left eyebrow rose as she stared back at Alan. She leaned into Alan and closed her eyes.

Alan leaned into her also, closed his eyes, and puckered up to kiss her, but ended up kissing her nose instead. They both laughed. He tried again, but with his eyes open this time, and successfully landed his lips on hers. Then he closed his eyes.

For both, the kiss seemed to last forever.

They jumped into Alan's car. He attempted to start it, but the engine would not turn over. He tried a couple more times, but all that did was result in a couple of backfires.

Alan looked over at Grace. He did not know if it was the radiant, golden light still surrounding her, or just her genuine beauty, but he leaned over and kissed her again.

The motor started as Alan ended his kiss.

They drove away in his mismatched 280Z. The sky brightened with the approaching new day. The golden light retreated below the rubble. Tony's Food Mart's neon sign was all that remained, standing in an empty parking lot, and a mound of rubble. The sign sparked a bit and then the lights died out.

THE END

I hope you enjoyed reading this book as much as I loved writing it. If you did, I would appreciate a short review on Amazon or your favorite book website. Reviews are crucial for any author and even just a short line or two can make a vast difference. Thank you.

V.C. Marello

Gate of Betrayal – Hell Gates series Book 2 – Coming in 2021

One year after Grace and Alan's escape from the clutches of the fallen angel, Samael, in San Francisco, the couple faces yet another Hell Gate supernatural phenomenon.

*"And then many will be offended,
will betray one another,
and will hate one another."
Matthew 24:10 NKJV*

ABOUT THE AUTHOR

V.C. Marello

What began as just a fascination with Friday late-night horror and Sci-Fi reruns, transformed itself and manifested in his imagination to ask "What If..." scenarios.

Fast-forward – he earned a Bachelor of Arts in Film Studies with an emphasis in screenwriting from San Francisco State University. His writing opportunities took him on a journey including his hometown's local PBS television station, writing press releases, and publishing winery reviews in the California Visitors Review. He was one of the writers for the employment comic book, *How to Get a Job and Keep It*, produced by the Sonoma County Business and Education Roundtable. One of his most enjoyable writing projects was working alongside historian, Nancy O'Sullivan-Beare, PhD.

where he completed the screenplay, *Witch of the Western Sea*, which earned an Honorable Mention from the Writer's Digest Magazine Writing competition.

His career took him into the technology field, married and raised a family. The "What if" scenarios persisted and evolved into stories. Now, those characters desire to reveal themselves to our world, no longer forgotten souls hidden in the shadows of an abandoned celestial plane of existence.

vcmarello@relativebooks.com

Author's Page:
https://www.relativebooks.com/authors.html

Made in the USA
Monee, IL
02 June 2021

69289452R00146